MONTANA RANGER
BROTHERHOOD PROTECTORS

BOOK #5

ELLE JAMES

New York Times & *USA Today*
Bestselling Author

Dedication

This story is dedicated to my youngest daughter who joined the Army National Guard and is proving to herself just how strong and competent she can be. She makes me so very proud.

Elle James

About This Book

Forced into medical retirement, Army Ranger Alex "Taz" Davila takes a job in the wilds of Montana with the Brotherhood Protectors. First assignment: undercover protection of a pretty physical therapist on a veteran's rehab ranch.

Living her dream job, Hannah Kendricks helps wounded warriors and abused horses at a rehab ranch for veterans. Finally in a position for a little romance, she suffers a setback when strange accidents nearly get her killed.

Her lagging libido gets a kickstart when a sexy new patient starts following her, always there when she turns around. Before long, she realizes he's the only thing standing between her and whoever is after her.

Accepting his offer to protect her, Hannah encounters a new problem. She's attracted to the man! Together they struggle to determine who wants to hurt her and why, while fighting the growing attraction they are helpless to resist.

Author's Note

If you enjoy reading about military heroes, read
other books in Elle James's **Brotherhood
Protector** and **Take No Prisoners Series**:

Brotherhood Protector Series
Montana SEAL (#1)
Bride Protector SEAL (#2)
Montana D-Force (#3)
Cowboy D-Force (#4)
Montana Ranger (#5)
Montana Dog Soldier (#6)
Montana SEAL Daddy (#7)

Take No Prisoners Series
SEAL's Honor (#1)
SEAL's Ultimate Challenge (#1.5)
SEAL's Desire (#2)
SEAL's Embrace (#3)
SEAL's Obsession (#4)
SEAL's Proposal (#5)
SEAL's Seduction (#6)
SEAL's Defiance (#7)
SEAL's Deception (#8)
SEAL's Deliverance (#9)

Visit www.ellejames.com for more titles and
release dates
For hot cowboys, visit her alter ego
Myla Jackson at www.mylajackson.com

Chapter 1

"Are you sure you don't want me to stay?" Gavin Blackstock straightened, after hooking up the mower to the oldest tractor on the Brighter Days Rehabilitation Ranch. He shook his shaggy black hair out of his gray eyes and wiped the grease from his hands.

Hannah Kendricks sighed. Yeah, she wished Gavin could stay and cut the hayfield instead of her, but...

"No, we need the supplies and tomorrow is Sunday. The feed stores are closed." She stared at the aging farm machinery, wondering if it would conk out in the middle of the field and leave her to walk all the way back to the barn. "I'll keep the tractor going long enough to cut the hay." She held up her hand as if being sworn into office. "Don't worry, I promise to baby it."

"Why don't you let Percy do the cutting?" Gavin suggested.

"I would, but he's better at manning the baler. The hay I cut three days ago is dry and ready to bale. If we want to get all of it baled by Wednesday, we need to cut today."

Gavin opened his mouth to protest.

Hannah held up her hand. "We've got it covered. I hired three hands to help."

"Troy Nash got here early this morning."

Gavin frowned. "Why did you hire that boy?"

"I heard he'd been fired from his job at the feed store. I figured he could use the money since his daddy had his heart attack."

"You've got a soft spot for those down and out."

She shrugged. "We take care of our neighbors in these parts."

"Yeah, but Troy's a known troublemaker."

"Maybe he just needs someone to believe in him." Hannah ran her hand across the smooth seat of one of the saddles stacked on a saddletree. "Besides, I hired Abe and Mark. They're good, hard-working teenagers. Don't worry about us."

"Why the hurry? If it doesn't get cut today, we can do it tomorrow when I'm here to help."

Glancing up at the bright Montana sky, Hannah shook her head. "A storm's headed our way from off the Washington coast. You know as well as I do that we can't bale it if it's wet. And if we don't cut the field now, the hay won't have time to dry and be baled before the storm hits."

"So?"

Hannah's lips tightened. "You know we need two cuttings from those fields to keep us from having to buy hay to get us through the winter."

Gavin glanced at the old tractor. "This hunk of junk gets crankier every time we use it. I brought it up to Holloway when he was here last month, but I'll mention it again. He's supposed to be here tomorrow."

Hannah bit down on her bottom lip.

Holloway was the young financial manager of the Brighter Days Rehabilitation Ranch. He showed up once a month to do the accounting and make any big buying decisions. Otherwise, he left the ranch for Hannah to run as she saw fit, making the day-to-day hiring, firing and maintenance decisions. "He can be pretty tight with the purse strings."

"Maybe you can turn on some of the charm you reserve for our clients." Gavin cocked his brows.

Hannah glanced down at her faded shirt and jeans and gave her best friend a very unladylike snort. "I'm not very convincing as a girl."

Gavin laughed out loud. "Don't knock yourself, Hannah. From where I stand, you're all female. And you do it better than most women I know."

"Yeah, but where Holloway comes from, I'm nowhere near the kind of woman he's used to dealing with. I don't even know how to bat my lashes." To prove it, she fluttered her eyelashes. The action felt as clumsy as it probably looked based on Gavin's grimace.

"Yeah, don't do that. It just looks weird." He limped to the truck. "Just try to be nice."

Hannah followed. "I'll see what I can do. We really need at least one newer tractor before next season." She hugged Gavin. "Thanks for giving it your best shot. At least, it's running."

"Hopefully, it will remain running until you get through the cutting." Gavin glanced toward

3

the barn. "Looks like Percy has his team of helpers ready. I'd better get to Eagle Rock and back so that I can be of some assistance before the day's over." He gave Hannah a stern glance. "Be careful out there. We don't want any more 'accidents'. We can't lose our best therapist."

"Your *only* therapist," Hannah muttered. "I'll be all right. Quit worrying. What happened recently was just a couple of accidents. They could have happened to anyone." She gripped Gavin's arm and stared directly into his eyes. "There's no conspiracy going on here at Brighter Days."

Frowning, he touched her cheek. "I'm not so sure. You're the only one the accidents have affected." He drew in a deep breath, released it and nodded. "I should stay and do the cutting."

"Go." Hannah gave Gavin a gentle shove. "I can handle this. And nobody is going to mess with me. I want to be here for the guys. Once I finish the field, I'll help load hay on the truck and trailer. I need to be there to watch and make sure none of them does anything that will set them back on their roads to recovery."

"Yes, you do need to be there. They wouldn't be nearly as far along as they are without your help." He glanced down at his leg. "I never thought I'd walk again, and look where I am, because of you."

Hannah's chest expanded. Nothing was more rewarding than helping wounded veterans regain mobility and some semblance of a life worth

4

living.

Working at the Brighter Days Rehab Ranch, she got the best of both worlds. She got to help people, like her best friend from childhood, and give former soldiers, sailors, Marines and airmen a reason to keep fighting, for a great cause— rehabilitating horses rescued from horrible situations.

And she wouldn't have had this opportunity if not for the benevolence of the investment group that had purchased the ranch and allowed her to make it into the thriving therapy center it was.

Gavin paused before climbing into the truck. "Oh, and Hannah, you might want to think about being the girl you are and date or find someone to love. You need a life outside of this ranch."

"Says the man who hasn't had a date in over a year?" She shook her head. "I'll date when you date." Narrowing her eyes, Hannah tilted her head. "Maybe I'll date you."

Gavin gave her a twisted smile. "Thanks, but it would be like dating my little sister. No can do."

Hannah nodded. They'd tried kissing, once, but the sparks weren't there and the connection didn't feel right. Like Gavin said, it was like kissing a sibling. Bleh! "You're right. We weren't made for each other in that way. Why spoil a perfect friendship? But that doesn't mean you can't find a woman to love you and all of your faults."

Gavin crossed his arms over his chest. "Same

to you, Han. Same to you. I'll date if you date."

"Watch what you dare. I've been known to rise to a challenge."

"I'm counting on it." He stood for a moment longer and then dropped his arms. "Go cut the hay, but don't forget...I dared you."

As Gavin climbed into the farm truck and spun around on the gravel, heading for town, Hannah watched, something tugged at her heart, telling her that Gavin had a point. Since she'd left college, she hadn't been on a date. Perhaps it was time.

Ranch foreman, Percy Pearson, appeared from around the side of the barn on the ranch's other tractor, towing the hay baler. He waved as he passed Hannah. "Ready?"

She nodded, climbed onto the old tractor's seat and waited for the farm truck, driven by medically retired Staff Sergeant Lori Mize, to pass. A motley crew of wounded warriors and hired hands filled the bed of the pickup, laughing and joking about the work ahead. She hoped between the group of able-bodied hired hands—Troy, Abe and Mark— and the three veterans—Franklin, Vasquez and Young, with their varying degrees of disabilities— they'd get the work done quickly.

Hannah started the engine and shifted the tractor into first gear. Resigning herself to a long day in the field, she adjusted her cowboy hat over her forehead and drove the tractor through the gate into the pasture. The clear sky promised to turn the cool Montana morning into a warm, early summer day. Hopefully, free of strange accidents.

Cookie, the ranch cook, waved and closed the gate behind her. He always stuck around for the warriors who weren't ready, or weren't capable of the heavy lifting needed to throw fifty- to eighty-pound hay bales onto the trailer. Not that they had any other veterans staying behind. All men and women were on deck that day. Cookie would have a huge meal waiting when they returned, tired and starving, having burned a ton of calories.

Hannah followed Percy until she came to the field she was to cut that day.

He pressed on to the one farther out, taking with him the truck with the crew that would load what he baled.

Hannah would spend the day alone, driving the tractor with the mower on the back. This particular field had its share of hills. She hoped and prayed the old tractor wouldn't bog down and give up while climbing the hills, and that the brakes would hold on the way down.

Starting at the far end with the steepest slopes, Hannah worked her way up and down the hill. She kept a steady pace, careful not to push the tractor's engine too hard. On the way down the hill, she moved as slowly as she could, shifting into low gear to let the engine help, rather than relying totally on the worn brakes.

After the first pass, she felt more confident the tractor would handle the job. She settled back in her seat and let her mind wander away from the hayfield.

Hannah thought about how far she'd come and how satisfied she was with where she'd landed in her life. Growing up on this ranch as the daughter of the owner's housekeeper, she'd learned to ride a horse almost before she'd learned to walk.

She'd never known her father. Her mother had instilled in her a love for the outdoors and ranch life. And she had all the male role models she needed to teach her what was expected of a man and how he should behave toward a woman. Preferring the outdoors to housework, Hannah had grown up working alongside the cowboys and ranch hands, doing everything they did to care for the animals, buildings and land.

Her mother had insisted she go to college, scrounging and saving so that her daughter wouldn't have to take out loans to pay for her tuition.

Hannah would rather have stayed at the ranch and worked with the horses, but she knew a college education meant a lot to her mother, so she'd gone.

Gavin, her best friend from high school, had joined the Marines and gone to fight in the Middle East. Two years into his enlistment, Gavin had been injured in battle, taking a hit to his leg. He'd come back to the States where he'd undergone multiple surgeries in an attempt to remove all the shrapnel, repair the damage and save the leg. Finally, they'd had to amputate below his knee. Once he'd lost his leg, he'd been fitted with a prosthetic and sent to rehabilitation therapy to learn how to deal with his loss. After several months, Gavin was medically retired and sent home where he struggled with depression and trying to fit into a place where he felt he no longer belonged.

Hannah had been on the fence about what to study. When she'd gone to visit her best friend in the hospital, and later in physical therapy, she'd made her decision. She wanted to help people like Gavin regain use of their limbs, or learn how to get along without them, and in the process, regain their independence, confidence and self-respect.

She'd studied hard so that she would be accepted into the physical therapy program and graduated at the top of her class. Her mother had been so proud.

She'd taken a position at a rehab center in Bozeman, working with people who'd had knee and hip replacements, rotator cuff surgeries and more. But she wanted to work with veterans.

Gavin had stayed in DC, looking for a job. He couldn't find anything that suited him. He liked being around horses more than people, but he still felt drawn to his comrades in the Marines, wishing he could be back in battle, helping to fight for his country.

Hannah had applied to work at Walter Reed in Bethesda, Maryland. The same day she'd received an invitation to interview, her mother had suffered a fatal stroke.

Though three years had passed, the pain of her loss still pinched Hannah's chest.

She pulled her mind out of her memories as she reached the end of the row. Turning the tractor, she started mowing the next row, heading down a hill toward a ravine lined with trees. The rhythmic chug of the engine lured her back into her memories.

Her mother died the day after her stroke, never having regained consciousness. Hannah had delayed her interview in Bethesda for two weeks to give herself time to arrange for her mother's funeral and to settle her affairs. She'd buried her mother, her only living relative, in the cemetery outside Eagle Rock, the nearest town to the ranch her mother had called home.

Percy and Gavin had stood by her side, along with the handful of ranch workers and the ranch owner, Mr. Lansing. They'd buried her mother on an ironically bright, sunny Montana day. She would have loved the sunshine.

In a domino effect, Mr. Lansing had a heart attack that night and ended up in a long-term care facility. Percy and Hannah knew the event was the beginning of the end of their little hodge-podge family of ranch workers.

Her heart heavy, Hannah had said her goodbyes to Gavin and the ranch hands. Then she'd entered the ranch house, packed up what she would keep of her mother's and arranged for the rest to be donated. Heartsick and so sad she could barely breathe, she'd set her suitcases by the front door, with the intention of leaving the ranch in the morning.

That's when Percy had come to her. Someone had asked to speak with her on the telephone.

She hadn't wanted to, but Percy insisted it was important—something to do with the sale of the ranch.

With a knife twisting in her heart, she'd taken the call. An attorney requested a meeting with her the following day. He had information about her mother's will and news about the sale of the ranch.

Reluctantly, she'd agreed to meet him at his office in Eagle Rock the next morning before she left town.

Hannah's lips lifted. Even from the grave, her mother had been looking out for her. She must have known the day would come soon when Mr. Lansing couldn't manage the ranch. He didn't have any heirs, and he'd need to sell. She'd left Hannah her life savings, a modest amount of money stashed away in the bank for her own retirement she'd never see. And she'd left a letter for Hannah.

Dear Hannah,

If you're reading this letter, I've managed to die before I had a chance to tell you about your father. I didn't talk to you about him as you grew up, but I wanted you to know he was a good man. I never told him about you, so don't blame him for not being a part of your life. Blame me. Maybe I didn't make the right decision by not telling you about him, but I felt it was the right one for you and for him. Just don't hate your father. And no matter what, I have always and will always love you with all of my heart. Love, Mom

Hannah barely heard the rest of what the lawyer had to say, so deep was she in her own misery.

He paused, expecting an answer to a question she hadn't absorbed.

Clutching the letter to her chest, she looked up and asked him to repeat it.

"Will you stay and help manage the transition from cattle ranch to a rehabilitation ranch for wounded warriors and sick or injured horses?"

Hannah blinked. "Who? Me?"

The lawyer nodded, repeating the proposition presented by the new owners of the ranch. "He—they want you to think about it." The lawyer leaned forward and touched her arm, his brows furrowed with obvious concern. "If you stay, the other employees will keep their jobs and you could do a whole lot of good for veterans and animals."

Stunned, she left his office in a daze and returned to the ranch where Percy met her with his duffel bag in hand.

He set down the bag and gripped her arms. "Hannah, are you okay?"

She nodded and then said, "Percy, I've been so wrapped up in my own grief, I didn't stop to think about you. What are you going to do when this ranch sells?"

He shrugged. "I don't know. I thought I'd head out to my sister's place in North Dakota."

"But you hate going to your sister's for more than a day...two tops."

"It's the only place I know to go." He forced a smile. "But don't worry about me. I always land on my feet."

She tilted her head and given him a stern stare. "You've worked here as long as I can remember. When was the last time you had to look for a job?"

He glanced away. "It's been about thirty years or so."

For the first time, Hannah noticed the gray in his brown hair and the deeply grooved lines around his eyes. The man had leathery skin from years in the sun and weather and he had to be closing in on sixty years old. Who would hire him?

Staring at her old friend, the man who'd been the closest thing to a father she'd had, Hannah had made her decision. "We're staying."

Her lips curled at the memory of Percy's expression when he realized he wouldn't have to go to his sister in North Dakota. She'd called Gavin the next day and begged him to come work for the Brighter Days Rehabilitation Ranch where he could help veterans and horses. He'd be doing his part for his brothers- and sisters-in-arms.

Hannah pressed her foot on the tractor's brakes as the hill dipped sharply toward the ravine. She'd made the turn on the previous pass with no problem.

But something snapped, making a clanking sound of metal hitting metal, and the brakes failed.

Hannah's heart jumped to her throat. Instead of slowing, the tractor picked up speed, the weight of the tractor plus the mower, pushing it even faster down the hill.

Hannah's fingers tightened on the steering wheel and her pulse raced. She debated turning to slow the vehicle in its headlong rush toward the ravine. But turning at that pace was a surefire way to flip the tractor.

She tried to shift to a lower speed to let the tractor engine slow her descent, but no matter how hard she shoved the lever, it wouldn't shift to low. Her gut clenched as she ran out of options.

With trees and rocks waiting for her to crash into them, Hannah had no other choice but to get off. Her only problem was, if she jumped, she stood a strong chance of landing in the mower. At which point she'd be cut to pieces.

She stared at the trees and rocks ahead, her mind working through the scenarios at lightning speed, survival instincts kicking in.

That's when she spotted her only chance. The option was risky, but slightly less risky than crashing into the ravine. She turned the tractor's steering wheel ever so slightly, careful not to cause it to flip, and angled it toward a large tree with a long branch hanging just low enough for her to reach out and snag it with her arms.

Hannah held on to the steering wheel, fighting to keep it headed toward the tree, wondering if she could pull off what she planned.

With no time left to change her mind, she released the steering wheel, pushed to her feet and threw both arms over the branch.

Her chest crashed into the solid limb, knocking the air from her lungs. But she held on.

The tractor and mower continued on their course straight toward a large boulder, smashing into it with enough force that the front end of the tractor crumpled. Momentum carried the mower forward, flipping it up and over the top of the tractor, crushing the seat where Hannah had sat moments before.

All of these actions happened in a matter of seconds. Hannah's arms slipped on the rough tree bark and she fell from her perch, landing on her back. Pain shot through her head and darkness enveloped her.

Chapter 2

Alex "Taz" Davila gripped his M4A1 rifle, holding it at the ready as his team infiltrated an Afghan village. On a mission to capture a member of the Taliban, they couldn't afford to fail. The team needed to bring him back to the intel guys for interrogation.

As the point man, Taz moved forward, building by building, to the one his sources indicated was where their target had last been seen.

Maintaining situational awareness of the surrounding buildings and rooftops, he moved slowly, slipping from shadow to shadow, careful to avoid detection.

Once he reached the correct mud-and-brick structure, he waited for the others to catch up and provide cover while he and three members of his team pushed through the door and into enemy-held territory.

They were working a highly sensitive operation. Army Intelligence had it from one of their informants that an American was syphoning weapons from shipments into the area of operations and selling them to the enemy.

The team's goal was to learn the name of the traitor and stop the flow of weapons into the enemy's hands.

Guthrie, Klingensmith and McCormick fell in beside him. Jones and Aguilera would swing around to take up positions on the sides of the building. Hix, one of their expert marksmen, would cover the rear to keep anyone from escaping out the back

"Ready?" Taz asked.

Each man of his infiltration team nodded, the men on the corners and in the rear replied via radio communication headsets. He trusted his infiltration team to have his back. They'd been through many raids together and knew the routine. Not that he didn't trust Hix, Jones and Aguilera, but they were replacements for the men lost to injury. Trust was key in any military operation. If you couldn't trust your team, you were screwed.

Taz was first to reach the building. The other three men plastered themselves against the walls beside him. The rest of the team took up defensive positions. On the finger-count of three, Taz kicked in the door and entered.

K-man followed and then McC and Guthrie. They searched room to room until they reached the last one in the back of the structure. Taz reached out to open the door. As he pushed it open, he saw movement inside. Something...someone was there. He could feel it. But he couldn't make out the shape in the dark interior. Then a face floated into view, materializing out of the shadows.

Behind him, gunfire sounded from outside the building. A hand rose from the room's shadowy interior and loosed a small, oval object. It bounced off Taz's leg, hit the ground and rolled into the room beside him.

"Grenade!" Taz yelled and threw himself away from the open doorway. An explosion knocked him off his feet. He fell, his head hitting hard on the stone floor, his helmet doing little to cushion the blow. The wall beside him erupted into projectiles and dust and then crashed down on top of him.

Then nothing. No pain, no sound, no light. Just a blessed, black abyss.

"Sir, you need to fasten your seatbelt in preparation for landing," a soft female voice said close to his ear.

Taz jerked awake and stared into the face of a woman wearing a navy-blue uniform. Her attire wasn't any military uniform he'd ever seen and he wasn't in an Afghan village, snorting dust into his lungs.

Blinking, he pushed himself upright in his seat and tried to remember where he was.

"Sir, you have to fasten your seatbelt before we land," the woman repeated.

"Land where?" he asked before he could stop himself. Slowly, the rumble of an engine registered in his hearing.

She smiled and shook her head. "In Bozeman, of course." Her brows rose up her forehead. "You *are* expecting to land in Bozeman, Montana, aren't you? Otherwise, you've come a long way on the wrong airplane." With a wink, she hurried to the forward galley where she secured the bag of trash she'd collected and took her own seat, buckling her belt across her lap and shoulders. She stared from her position facing the cabin full of passengers, a smile curling the corners of her lips.

He glanced around at the interior cabin of the regional aircraft. Pain lanced through his head. Once again, he'd temporarily forgotten where he was and why he was there. He buckled his safety belt and pinched the bridge of his nose. Trying to remember his dream.

The psychologist said his chances of getting back his memory of the attack three months after his head injury were slim. Familiar anger roiled in his gut. Frustration filled him every time he dreamed about his last mission in the theater of operations. He'd been the only survivor of the four men who'd entered the building, and only because whoever had been shooting at the team presumed him dead.

Taz hadn't regained consciousness until he was in Germany at the military hospital at Landstuhl. He couldn't talk, nor could he move his arms or legs like he used to. Oh, he wasn't paralyzed, but the traumatic brain injury had scrambled his memory. For the first few days, he'd felt trapped in his body. All he could do was stare up at the lights over his bed and wish he were dead.

And worse, a man from CID has been there when he woke. What would the Army Criminal Investigations Division want with him? It wasn't like he'd committed a crime. When the man discovered Taz couldn't form words, he asked questions that only needed a yes or no answer. It had been a blur. Taz couldn't remember the questions he'd been asked or the answers he'd given.

From Landstuhl, he'd been airlifted to Bethesda, Maryland, where he'd spent the past three months relearning how to walk, talk, feed and dress himself. The first few weeks had been hell. On multiple occasions, he'd railed at God, wishing he had died a warrior's death with his team. Instead, he was forced to endure the humiliation of being taught how to hold a spoon like a two-year-old.

Harnessing his anger, he relearned old skills quickly, determined not to be a burden on society. By the time he'd left the rehabilitation center, he was jogging two to three miles on the treadmill and grunting out a hundred pushups and sit-ups in less than two minutes each.

Almost back to normal physically, he'd gone before the Army Medical Review Board. Because of his traumatic brain injury, they'd deemed him incapable of returning to active duty.

Though he didn't want to leave the army, Taz knew his discharge was probably for the best. Logic told him his mind wasn't what it had been.

Hell, he had missing memories, and he couldn't remember much of what had happened since he'd been pulled from the rubble of the building. He couldn't remember what he'd seen in that last room, nor could he remember the face of the man who'd pulled the pin on the grenade and tossed it into the hallway where Taz and his buddies had been standing.

As part of conducting an after action report, a couple of men from military intelligence had interviewed him in Maryland. They'd shared that the mission that had ended his career had failed. The team hadn't captured the Taliban leader who could have helped them identify the American responsible for selling weapons to the enemy.

Bottom line, Taz and his battle buddies had sacrificed everything for nothing. The traitor was still alive.

Thus, Taz's fervent desire to remember something from that day. Anything that would point to who might have tipped off the Taliban to their operation. Whose face had he seen before the grenade exploded? He felt like he should know the man he'd seen in the shadows, but no matter how hard he tried, he couldn't remember his features.

From what he'd learned from the team who'd been outside the building, they'd been fired on from above. Both Jones and Aguilera had taken hits. Hix had helped them get out of the line of fire and radioed for support. The man had been decorated and labeled a hero for getting the two injured rangers out alive.

The Taliban leader they'd been intent on capturing had been gone for hours. The men their leader had left in place had opened fire and dropped a concussion grenade before hightailing it out of the building through a tunnel that ran under the village to a point on the perimeter, outside the town's walls.

They still didn't have a handle on who was supplying weapons and who'd alerted the Taliban to their raiding party.

K-Man, McC and Guthrie died in the explosion that knocked out Taz. But he'd lived. When the recovery team came in to collect the bodies, they'd been surprised to find him still alive, buried beneath the rubble.

The airplane slowed and the pilot deployed the landing gear. Moments later, the tires skimmed the tarmac and the aircraft eased into one of the terminal gates.

As soon as the fasten seatbelt lights extinguished, Taz released the buckle and stood, working the kinks out of his sore muscles. He wasn't exactly sure what happened next or if he would be staying long in Montana. But, given Hank's job offer had been the only one he'd received, he figured it wouldn't hurt to check out the Brotherhood Protectors.

If he learned this was some vigilante neighborhood watch group, he'd turn right around and get back on the airplane.

To where?

His new employer had bought out the remainder of the lease on his apartment in Bethesda. His therapist had told him he was capable of continuing his exercise routine on his own. He didn't need a physical or occupational therapist anymore. Taz wasn't sure about leaving Dr. Rimmer, his mental health therapy leader. Until his memory returned and he quit having bouts of extreme anger and blinding headaches, he wouldn't feel back to 100 percent.

At least, he'd be out of the metro D.C. area. He'd never liked living in the city. And after nearly getting run over twice and almost being killed in a drive-by shooting, he was ready to be in the wide-open spaces of Montana where he might get some peace and quiet.

Hopefully, Montana wouldn't have as many drivers with road rage, bent on plowing through people on the sidewalks to get to where they were going. And he bet they didn't have as many drive-by shootings. He might have time to sort through his memories and get his head on straight.

The passengers in front of him pulled suitcases and backpacks from the overhead bins, reminding Taz to collect his own case. Like a steer being let through the chutes at an auction barn, Taz walked through the narrow aisle between the seats and down the steps onto the tarmac.

Once inside the terminal, he followed the signs leading to the baggage claim area where he was to meet with Hank Patterson, the owner/operator of the business. Taz hoped he'd be able to tell him more about what was expected of him as an agent for Brotherhood Protectors. From his phone interview with Patterson, he got the impression he would be some kind of bodyguard, or high-dollar babysitter.

It was a job. He didn't have a herd of employers knocking at his door to offer him anything else.

For as long as he could remember, he'd wanted to be an Army Ranger. He figured he'd be in the army until the day he died. The big glitch was when he didn't die in that explosion.

Now, out of the army and forced into the civilian world, he had no clue what he wanted to do, or what job he was qualified for. Not many companies were interested in expert marksmen or a man skilled in demolitions.

Hank Patterson's call had come at a most opportune time. Taz had been released from rehab. He had just been online, creating a pathetic excuse for a resume when he'd received the call from the former Navy SEAL. The man had thrown him a lifeline.

Hell, if a SEAL could make a successful transition into the civilian world, why couldn't Taz?

So, he'd accepted the position, packed his shit and hopped on the plane for Montana. Having grown up on a ranch in south Texas, Taz wasn't so sure what to expect in the cold north. Except the temperatures would probably bite in the winter like it had in the mountains and hills of Afghanistan.

As he stepped into the baggage claim area, he glanced around, searching for someone who looked like he ate nails for a snack and could twist off a man's head with his bare hands.

A cowboy wearing a blue chambray shirt and scuffed boots stepped forward, eyes narrowing. "Davila?"

Taz nodded. "Patterson?"

The cowboy smiled and held out a hand. "Glad to meet you, finally. I've been tracking your progress at Bethesda, waiting for your release."

Taz frowned. "You were tracking my progress? Isn't that a violation of some health privacy act?"

Shaking his head, the man shrugged. "I have a network of friends—current and former military. One of the guys from my old SEAL team went through Bethesda." He held up a hand. "It's been a year or so. You wouldn't have run into him, but you might have run into his wife, a therapist by the last name of Nipton."

Taz tipped his head. "Compact blond with a mean streak? About so high?" He raised a hand to shoulder level.

"That's her." Hank chuckled. "She was a cop in her first career. Tough as nails, but a heart of gold."

A smile slipped across Taz's face. "Yeah, she whipped my butt in shape. Reminded me of my drill sergeant in basic combat training." His lips turned downward, his gut twisting. He didn't like being spied on. "Was she feeding you information from my medical record?" Nor did he like the idea of anyone but his mental health therapist knowing he had issues remembering and keeping his cool. He'd come a long way from when he'd awakened in the hospital, but he felt like he had a long way yet to go.

"She didn't tell me specifics. Leigha was the one who alerted me to your potential as a Brotherhood Protector. She's really good about helping her patients move on after therapy. And she knew I was on the lookout for highly-skilled combat veterans I can trust to take on stateside missions."

Patterson followed Taz to the luggage

carousel. When he tried to take the duffel bag, Taz stopped him.

"Let's be clear," Taz said. "I can carry my own weight. I'm nearly back to 100 percent physical strength."

Smiling, Patterson held up his hands. "No offense intended. If you want to carry your gear, I'm not stopping you."

Realizing he might have come across too strong or angry, Taz toned down his voice. "Thanks, I appreciate your help, but like Mrs. Nipton told me over and over, *Don't rely on anyone else to do the things you should do for yourself.*"

"Good advice. Speaking of therapists." Patterson led the way out of the terminal. "I hope you didn't get too much of them at Walter Reed." He stopped beside a four-wheel drive black pickup.

Taz froze halfway through tossing his duffel into the back. "Why do you ask?"

"Because I already have an assignment for you."

Still holding onto his duffel bag, Taz stared at Patterson, his eyes narrowing. "I'm listening."

"I need you as a covert operative at the Brighter Days Rehab Ranch."

"Covert?" He lifted the bag and laid it in the bed of the truck. Despite his initial reticence at being a glorified babysitter, Taz was intrigued by the aspect of being covert.

"I need you to go to the ranch as a wounded warrior there for therapy."

His hackles rising, Taz's eyes tightened into slits. "You're not bull-shitting me are you? I'm done with therapy. If you think I need more before I take on a real assignment, I'm out of here."

Anger roiled beneath the surface. He could feel the heat rising in his chest and up his neck. Taking in a long deep breath through his nose, he let it out slowly, like his mental health therapist had taught him. The heat abated a little.

Patterson chuckled. "No. You and I know you're physically fit for this assignment, but the therapist at the ranch won't know that. And *she's* your assignment."

Tension easing a little, Taz flexed his shoulders. "What do you mean she's my assignment?"

"I have an undisclosed client who hired us to protect the therapist at Brighter Days Rehab Ranch. He's willing to pay good money to keep her safe."

"From what? Disabled veterans?"

"Several attempts have been made on her life. If you ask her, she brushes them off as accidents, but her benefactor believes otherwise."

"Who is her benefactor?"

"He refused to say. Money was wired from a foreign bank account to cover our services. I have my computer guy working on tracing it, but in the meantime, the therapist at the ranch could be in danger. And since you're available and the most recent of my agents to be in therapy, you're the logical choice to place on this assignment. The question is…are you up for it?" Patterson's chin lifted and he crossed his arms over his chest.

What choice did Taz have? He'd accepted the job to work for Brotherhood Protectors. How hard could it be to follow a therapist around a ranch?

"I'd take it myself," Patterson said. "But I have a new baby at the house, and my wife wouldn't be too happy if I don't pull a few night shifts with Emma. You know…happy wife, happy life."

Never having been married or even considered tying the knot, Taz didn't know. "I'm up for it. When do I start?"

"You're going there now."

Holy shit. Taz schooled his face into an emotionless mask. He hadn't expected to be thrown right in without recon or an intel briefing. "I'm new to this protection agency business. What do I do?"

"Follow the client, maintain situational awareness. Figure out who might have it in for her and neutralize the source."

"Neutralize? As in taking them out?" Taz shook his head. "This is the U.S. The last I knew killing someone was illegal, unless in self-defense."

"I'm not telling you to kill someone. I'm asking you to make sure our client isn't killed. You're an Army Ranger. From my intel, I hear you're one of the best."

He stiffened and his gut burned. "*Was.*" Until he walked into a trap. Now, he couldn't remember enough details about it to identify those responsible.

"So, you were injured. You're walking on your own two feet. That's better than some veterans you'll meet at the ranch."

"I'm lucky to be alive and with all four limbs still attached." Taz shoved a hand through his hair and sighed. "Or so they say."

Patterson touched a hand to Taz's shoulder and spoke softly, "Sometimes living is harder than dying. Especially when you're the only one of your team to make it through. And not all wounds are visible. Some of them are deep inside." He laid a hand over his chest. "If you need anything, I'm always a phone call away. *If* you can get cell phone reception. I recommend finding a landline. I'll be around, and I'll come or send help, if you need it."

His chest tightening, Taz swallowed at the sudden lump in his throat. "Thanks."

Patterson turned and held open the driver's door to the shiny black pickup. "I programmed the GPS. It'll take you right to the Brighter Days Rehab Ranch."

Taz stared at Patterson and at the open driver's door. "Aren't you coming?"

Patterson shook his head. "Nope. You're a returning soldier destined for the rehab facility. I've had my computer guy hack their system and slip in your chart, with the arrival date as today."

His new boss handed him the truck key. Taz wrapped his fingers around the fob.

"You'll find weapons, ammo and protective gear behind the back seat. Feel free to use any or all. Any questions?" Patterson asked.

"What's my client's name?"

"Hannah Kendricks." The Navy SEAL shut the door and stepped back.

Taz slipped the key into the ignition and cranked the engine. The powerful four-wheel drive pickup roared to life. Depressing a button, he lowered the window. "Do you need a ride somewhere?"

Patterson grinned and nodded farther down the side of the runway. "My ride is over there."

When Taz turned to look, he noticed a sleek black helicopter outside a hangar, with a man circling the outside with a clipboard.

For a former SEAL, Hank Patterson had some major connections. Taz prayed they were all legal. He'd hate to think his new employer hired former military to conduct illegal ops.

Forcing back his misgivings, Taz followed the directions on the GPS. Once at the ranch, he'd stick with the therapist like an insect to fly paper. Following one woman around a ranch would be a piece of cake.

Chapter 3

One day lying around the house, recovering from her close call with death, had Hannah climbing the walls. She'd argued with Percy and Gavin, stating a few bumps and bruises weren't sufficient reason to be placed under house arrest. After moaning and complaining for all to hear, she'd managed to cajole her jailors into loosening their hold and letting her return to work.

Hannah leaned through the tack room door. "What did you do with those fence staples you picked up in town yesterday?"

Gavin glanced up from the table where he'd been working on the leather strap to replace one that had been damaged on a ranch saddle. "On the shelf behind me. Why?"

Hannah entered, locating the plastic bucket with the horseshoe-shaped nails. "I'm tackling the fence the bull mauled the other day."

"I was going to do that. If you wait until I finish this strap, I'll get it done."

"I can do it." She waved her hand. "Take your time on that strap. That particular saddle is my favorite, and you're much better at leatherwork than I."

A young man ducked his head around the doorframe. "Miss Kendricks, Vasquez and I finished pouring the feed into the bins. What's

31

next?"

Hannah turned to Brody Franklin, a blond-haired, green-eyed young man and one of her clients. She refused to call them patients. They had finished their therapy at the military hospitals and were at Brighter Days to regain their confidence and an understanding of just how much they *could* do, even when missing an arm, a leg or both.

In Franklin's case, he'd lost his dominant right arm. He'd had to relearn how to dress himself, write left-handed and complete all of the functions he'd performed with his right hand before he'd lost it due to an attack in Afghanistan that nearly cost him his life. At the ripe young age of nineteen, he'd been depressed and unhappy about returning home. He'd been afraid his family would be too clingy, and that he'd never fit back into his old life.

When they'd opened the ranch for clients, Hannah had reached out to one of the therapists who'd worked with Gavin at Walter Reed, letting him know of the program at Brighter Days. The therapist had recommended the program to Franklin.

Happy to delay his trip home, Franklin had jumped at the opportunity to go to Montana.

On the same plane, he'd met Xavier Vasquez, a young Marine a year older who'd suffered a similar loss of his left arm. They'd been at Brighter Days for a week, just beginning to learn how to live again.

Hannah had been fairly easy on them, giving them tasks she knew they could accomplish with one arm. Time to give them a little more of a challenge. "I want you and Vasquez to muck the stalls."

Franklin frowned. "Muck stalls?"

"Yes. Rake all of the old straw and manure from the stalls, dump it in the compost pile outside the back of the barn and spread new straw on the floors of the stalls."

"How the hell—"

Looking over his shoulder, Gavin glared at the young man.

Franklin immediately clamped his lips shut. "Sorry. Miss Kendricks, how are we supposed to use a rake with one arm?"

Hannah raised her brows and tilted her head. "You and Vasquez are pretty smart. I'm sure you'll find a way."

Franklin opened his mouth to protest. One glance at Gavin and he snapped it shut. "Yes, ma'am." The former soldier executed an about face and went to find Vasquez.

"How will they manage a rake?" Gavin asked.

Hannah shrugged. "They'll have to figure that out for themselves. They need to learn where there's a will, there's a way. The only thing limiting them is their attitude. Other clients have done it before."

Gavin's lips twitched. "You always seem to know how best to deal with the new recruits."

If she could, Hannah would have hugged

each one of their clients and sheltered them from any hurt or harm. But they had to learn how to handle life on their own. Surrounded by other people in similar situations, they could try and fail and try again without fear of being laughed at.

Brighter Days was a place they could learn just how much they could do and that they still had value. Each person who came to Brighter Days had to help with the rescue horses. By helping someone or something other than themselves, the clients learned they had worth and could do good. Eventually, they'd know how they could fit into society.

"How was the call to Mr. Moneybags?" Gavin asked.

The question brought her back to ground and her current worries. Hannah sighed. "Holloway wasn't too happy about the loss of the tractor."

Gavin faced her, a deep frown descending on his brow. "What do you mean he wasn't happy about losing the tractor? We almost lost *you*." He turned, giving her his full attention. "We can replace a tractor. We can't replace you."

"Sure you can," Hannah assured him. "You'd just have to hire another therapist."

Gavin set aside the strap and stood. "You're crazy." He gripped her arms and shook her gently. "You're not replaceable in my mind."

"Yeah, but I am replaceable in Holloway's." She leaned against Gavin's chest. "I do wish he could have seen the accident from my point of view. I don't know what would have happened if that tree hadn't been there, or hadn't had a branch hanging low enough for me to catch a ride on."

"It wasn't an accident," Gavin argued. "I'd checked those brakes the day before, and the engine the morning it happened."

"Yeah, but the tractor was getting old."

"No buts." He hugged her. "After you nearly bit the big one, I went down to the wreckage and checked them again. The brakes were sabotaged. I'd swear on a Bible that it was so."

"Why?" She looked up at her best friend's face, at a complete loss and frustrated with a situation she couldn't control. "What have I done to make anyone want to kill me?"

Gavin shook his head. "I don't know. But it has to stop. Before you're hurt any more than you already have been. Maybe you should stay in the house until we figure out who's doing this."

Hannah pushed away from Gavin and pressed a hand to one of her bruised ribs. She winced. "No way. Too many people and animals rely on me to help them through the rough times. I won't let them down."

"Yeah, while you're out helping others, you're putting your life and the people around you at risk." Gavin raised his brows. "Have you thought about that?"

Hannah didn't mind so much that *she'd* been targeted three times, but if someone took a hit because he or she was standing next to her, she could never forgive herself. "Maybe you're right.

Being around the clients while someone has it in for me could put them in unnecessary danger." She chewed on her bottom lip, thinking through the possibilities. "Perhaps I should hang back from our clients. I'd hate for one of them to get hurt because of me."

"I'd hate for you to get hurt." Lowering to the seat, Gavin rubbed his knee.

Hannah frowned. "Still having phantom pain?"

Gavin shoved his knees beneath the table he'd been working on. "It's fine."

"Have you tried using the mirror I gave you?" she asked, pretty sure of the answer.

"No. The whole idea seemed too ridiculous." Gavin retrieved the leather strap and went back to punching holes through the middle. "The pain isn't real anyway." His voice turned harsh and his lips tightened.

"Gavin, your pain is real. You have to retrain your brain from getting mixed signals. Mirror therapy has been proven to work. Didn't it help you that one day we tried it?"

Gavin wouldn't look up, but he finally responded, "The pain went away. But how do you know the reason was the mirror therapy and not just that the pain subsided?"

"Try the mirror again. And again. If it continues to work, what does it hurt to keep doing the therapy?"

"What's the use? The leg isn't going to grow back."

"No, but you don't need it to grow back in order to get on with your life. Gavin, you've been back for a couple years. You need to put yourself out there and date."

He looked up at her. "What woman will want half a man?"

Her chest tightened. She hated seeing the pain in Gavin's eyes. "You're not half a man. You're a wonderful, intelligent, strong man who can do anything a man with two legs can do. Only better."

"How so?"

"You have a heart twice as big as any man I know. You care about animals, and you care about people. Any woman would want a man like that in her life. Hell, I'd be happy to have you in my life, but we're too much like brother and sister. You'd be settling for second best. You'd only want to be with me because you're comfortable around me."

"What's wrong with that?"

Hannah rolled her eyes. "Remember that time we kissed in high school?" She shuddered. "Admit it, the kiss didn't do anything for you, either. I remember you even told me so. And then you went panting after Lisa Preston, the cheerleader."

Gavin grinned, his gray eyes sparkling in the early morning sunshine. "Yeah. She was something."

"And I was chopped liver?" Hannah propped a fist on her hip.

Gavin shook his head. "No. But the spark wasn't there. I felt like I'd committed incest, kissing my sister, even though we're not related."

"Exactly." She brushed her lips across his forehead. "You deserve to find the love of your life, get married and have a houseful of kids."

He snorted. "Which brings us back to the conversation we had the other day. When are you going to start dating?"

"Soon. I think I'm finally to a point in my work here that I can take a little time for myself." She straightened and looked around at the neat and clean tack room. "Percy works wonders keeping the ranch on schedule and maintaining the buildings. You're incredible with the horses and the clients. I think I can take a little time off every once in a while."

Gavin nodded, a smile spreading. "Want me to set you up with someone?"

Hannah frowned. "Hell no. I can find my own man."

"Oh, yeah?" Gavin's eyes narrowed. "Where?"

"I don't know. I'm sure he'll turn up when I'm least expecting him, and I'll fall madly in love. We'll get married and have a dozen children to play with your houseful." She lifted the bucket of nails and started to turn.

"Still think you should let me fix you up," Gavin persisted. "At least then I'd know he was good enough for you."

She loved Gavin for saying so, but still…"I'd

rather do it my way."

"That could take forever."

"Who knows?" Hannah smiled, hoping to lighten the subject of dating. "My man might be the next person who walks through that door."

Arching an eyebrow, Gavin leaned to his left and looked around her, which made Hannah turn, her pulse kicking up a notch.

The doorway remained empty.

She let go of the breath she'd been holding and laughed at herself. "It will happen when it happens. Until then, I have a fence to mend." She shot a smile back at Gavin and swung around, heading for the exit, and ran into a wall of muscles.

The collision made her let go of the bucket. The plastic hit the ground, the lid popped off and fence staples spilled onto the floor. "Oh, for heaven's sake." She bent at the same time a man did and they knocked skulls.

Pain shot through her forehead and she sat back on her bottom. "Oh!"

The man she'd bumped into rocked back on his feet and sat down hard. His eyes glazed, and he swayed more than she did.

Hannah pushed past her own pain and leaned up on her knee, a staple piercing the fabric of her jeans. She didn't care.

The man in front of her paled. He appeared like he was about to pass out.

"Hey." She grabbed his arm and held him steady. "Are you all right?"

He nodded and pressed the fingers of both hands to his temples. "I'm fine," he said, in clipped tones. When he dropped his hands, the haze in his eyes cleared, replaced by a concerned frown. "Did I hurt you?"

She shook her head, the pain receding.

He looked at the mess on the floor. "I'm sorry. I'll get these." He scooped up a handful of staples and deposited them into the plastic bucket.

Hannah came up on her haunches and helped collect the nails. In a couple of minutes, they'd secured all of the staples in the tub.

The man rose with the bucket, swayed a bit and then steadied.

Hannah straightened and held out her hand. "I'll take those."

He surrendered the container. "Please, accept my apologies."

"No, it was my fault." She twisted her lips into a crooked smile. "I should watch where I'm going. Can I help you?"

"I'm looking for a Hannah Kendricks." He stared into her face. "I don't suppose that would be you?"

Hannah stared up into the deepest, darkest eyes she'd ever seen. The man towered over her, his shoulders impossibly broad and his face ruggedly handsome. What had he asked? Oh, yeah. "I'm Hannah. And you are?"

The man held out his hand. "Alex Davila. My therapist told me I might see if you had room for one more patient here at the Brighter Days Rehab

Ranch."

Hannah's heartbeat sped as she took the proffered hand. "Man or beast?" Holy smokes she couldn't help staring at the beast in front of her and all of his sexy maleness.

His lips quirked upward. "Man." He touched his chest. "Although, I've been called a beast by some of my friends. The patient would be me."

The wind sucked out of her chest, Hannah felt as if her lungs had deflated to completely empty of all oxygen. "You?" She ran her gaze over him from the top of his cowboy hat to his sexy new cowboy boots. "Actually, we do have room at the ranch."

"Oh, good. When they turned me loose at Walter Reed, I wasn't sure where I'd go next. I was getting close to pre-injury normal, but I didn't want to backslide." He gave her a smile. "Would you consider taking me on? I hear you have a good program here."

"You have?" The fact that he would be one of the ranch's clients made her feel both disappointed and relieved all at once.

As a client, he would be strictly off limits to her personally. Hannah had an ironclad rule for herself. Don't get involved with the patients. Er…clients. They needed to learn to function on their own. Falling for their therapist would only delay their re-entry into society. Shaking off the need to lick the man from head to toe, Hannah swallowed hard and took his hand. "Alex, you say?"

He nodded. "My friends call me Taz."

"It wouldn't happen to be short for Tasmanian Devil, would it?"

He grinned.

The action lit a fire at Hannah's core.

"Guilty," Taz said.

"Let me guess," she said, her words tripping on her suddenly heavy tongue. "You're the kind of person who spins into a situation, stirs it up and spins back out before anyone realizes what hit them?" Like he had her heart and her head spinning right then.

He shrugged. "Something like that."

"What would you like us to call you? Alex, Davila or Taz?"

"Taz will do." He stared down at her hand in his. "Do you mind if I have that back?"

Heat rushed up into her cheeks as she realized she'd been holding the client's hand all the time they'd been discussing his name. Hannah yanked her hand out of his, suddenly missing the warmth and strength. Which was ridiculous. She didn't need either. But knowing that didn't stop her from wanting them...

Hannah squared her shoulders, determined to be professional amid her totally *unprofessional* thoughts. "Gavin will show you to the bunkhouse and get you settled in. But before you decide to stay, you should know, everyone who comes here is expected to pull his or her own weight in one form or another. Disabilities aren't an excuse to get out of working. The animals we rescue count on us to make their lives better."

Taz's brows dipped. "I thought this was a rehab ranch for veterans."

"And horses. We also rescue abused and mistreated horses. The veterans who come to us learn that they're not the only living creatures with seemingly insurmountable problems. Our charges help each other heal." She tipped her head in challenge. "Are you willing to do your share?"

He nodded. "I am."

"Have you ever been around horses?" she asked.

Taz's lips twitched. "A little."

Hannah suspected he wasn't telling the whole truth. However, she had work to do, and standing around drooling over a client wasn't getting it done. "As I said, Gavin will show you to your quarters." She left the tack room as quickly as she could without appearing bitchy or off-putting. Being near Taz was making her insides burn and her thoughts scramble.

"Hey! What the hell!" a voice shouted.

Hannah recognized it as Franklin's.

"You got it on me first, you damned grunt," Vasquez responded.

A snort sounded from the other side of a stall and something sailed into the air, landing with a plop on the ground at Hannah's feet.

"Rather be a grunt than a jarhead," Franklin shouted.

"Yeah, at least the shit is on the outside of my boots, not on the inside," Vasquez said.

Two more clumps of straw-studded horse manure sailed out of the stall, landing on the ground near Hannah.

"What's going on in there?" she shouted, anger building as yet another clump of manure flew out of the stall.

"He started it," Franklin said, and grunted.

Hannah ran toward the stall, afraid the two young men would hurt each other with the hay rakes.

When she reached the stall gate, she stopped, her lips twitching, laughter bubbling up inside. Franklin and Vasquez were in a war of the rakes, balancing the two tools beneath their good arms, using their bodies to apply leverage. The rake tines were locked, and they were at a standoff.

Then Franklin backed off, dug his tines into the straw and manure and slung shit at Vasquez.

Vasquez ducked, and the horse manure hit Hannah in the chest. She let out a sharp breath and backed up a step.

The two fighters froze, their eyes rounding.

"Miss Kendricks, I'm so sorry." Franklin ran toward her, still carrying his rake.

"It's okay," Hannah said, choking on her sudden need to giggle. She tried not to let it out. The situation was serious, but the guys covered in crap looked hysterically funny. She couldn't hold back and let loose a bark of laughter.

"Attention!" a commanding voice said behind her. "Drop your tools."

Both men quickly dropped their rakes and

stood straight.

"It's okay." Hannah stopped laughing long enough to take a deep breath. When she did, she smelled the manure on her shirt and made a belated attempt to brush it off. Then, to make certain Franklin didn't devolve into another brawl later, she schooled her face into a stern mask and faced them. "You do realize you're cleaning up the mess you made?"

The two spoke as one, "Yes, ma'am!"

She tilted her chin a little higher. "And what did you learn today while slinging manure all over the barn?"

Their brows descended. "Ma'am?" Franklin questioned.

"Not to sling shit because it's wrong?" Vasquez guessed.

"That, too." Hannah let her lips curl into a smile as she gestured toward the vets. "More importantly, you learned you could manage a rake with one hand. And you did well enough to sling a considerable amount of manure all over the place. Now that you know you can do that, you can put your backs into cleaning up."

"Yes, ma'am!" Franklin and Vasquez said as one. But they didn't move. Their gazes shifted to the man who'd commanded them to attention.

"Get to it," Taz said, his voice deep, strong and brooking no argument.

Franklin and Vasquez scrambled for the rakes. Each grabbed a handle on the wheelbarrow. Together they rolled it toward the middle of the barn and started shoveling manure.

Gavin stood at the tack room door, chuckling. "You should probably get a shower, before anything else"

"I'll shower when I'm done working outdoors," she responded sharply.

"At least let me get it out of your hair." Taz raised his hand and paused with it poised above her hair. "Do you mind?"

She shook her head, her gaze fixed on his eyes.

Taz stood so close, she could see the individual stubble on his chin and tiny flecks of gold in his deep brown eyes. Then her gaze shifted to his full, sensuous lips, and her breath caught in her throat.

Her newest client reached out to flick a straw from her hair. "There."

"Good thing Davila *walked through the door* when he did," Gavin muttered. "Saved me some time." He winked.

Gavin's emphasis on *walked through the door* shook Hannah out of her staring stupor and brought her back to the ground on her own two feet. "I don't know what you're talking about."

Oh, she did, but she didn't want Gavin to spell it out. How embarrassing would it be if Gavin told Taz she'd made a joke that the next man who walked through the door would be her one true love, the man she'd marry and spawn a dozen children with?

Even the thought of that kind of humiliation

caused heat to rise up her neck and burn across her cheeks. She turned her head away from Taz.

"I'll gladly tell you what I'm talking about," Gavin said, grinning.

"Save it," she cut him off with a glare. "Aren't you supposed to be showing our new guest where he can stow his gear?"

"Going." Gavin tossed the leather strap he was holding back into the tack room and waved a hand toward the door. "Davila?"

Taz nodded.

Gavin left the room and the barn.

As Taz turned to leave, he paused for a moment in front of Hannah. "I liked the way you handled the boys."

She shrugged, though the compliment made her feel warm all over. "They can do so much more than they give themselves credit for. And sometimes it's okay if they fight and squabble. As long as they don't hurt each other. They need a release for their frustration."

The client raised his hand toward her temple.

Unable to move, Hannah held her breath, waiting for his touch. She could almost feel the warmth of his skin on hers.

Instead of touching her cheek, he reached higher and plucked a straw from her hair. "You might want to get that shower." He smiled and left her standing there.

Hannah waited a full minute before she released the breath that had been trapped in her chest. *Holy hell.* The man's smile had practically turned her legs to jelly. The situation was bad. *Really bad.* How could she be a good therapist to a man when all she wanted to do was press her body against his and feel all of those lovely, bulging muscles beneath her fingertips?

She shook herself. What was wrong with her? Had she gone too long without purely male companionship? Or was her behavior from the lack of sex?

Sweet Jesus! Nothing good would come of following her insane desire.

Chapter 4

"By the way, I'm Gavin Blackstock." The man Hannah had sent Taz with stopped outside the barn and stuck out his hand.

Taz took it and gave it a firm shake. When he went to let go, the other man's grip tightened.

"Look, Hannah is one of the best people around. She has a heart bigger than the state of Montana and would do anything for anyone."

Taz pulled his hand out of Blackstock's and let the blood rush back into his fingers. "That's good to know."

"I'm telling you this, because I wouldn't take kindly to anyone hurting her."

"Message received. I don't plan on doing her any harm, if that's what you're worried about." Hell, he was there to protect her. He fought a grin.

Blackstock's eyes narrowed. "There's more ways than one to injure someone. Hannah means a lot to me. If anyone causes her grief, they'll have to answer to me."

"Maybe I'm not seeing the problem here." Taz shot a glance toward Blackstock. "I'm not here to hurt your woman."

The man's eyes widened. "Hannah? My woman?" He shook his head and chuckled. "She'd laugh you from here to tomorrow. No, she's more like a sister to me." His mouth twisted and he studied Taz. "And if she was to take a liking to someone, I'd do the brotherly thing and make sure he did right by her."

Taz held up his hands. "You don't have to worry about me. I'm not in the market for your sister."

"Yeah? Well, good." Blackstock was silent for a long moment. "My warning aside…if you *were* interested in her, and she returned the feeling, I might be willing to back off a little."

"Seriously, my relationship with Miss Kendricks will be on a strictly professional basis." He couldn't get caught up in her blue eyes and her soft laughter. He was there on a mission.

Blackstock seemed to chew on Taz's words. "Well, don't discount her just because she had a little horse manure in her hair. She cleans up pretty well." He turned and headed toward the sprawling ranch house up a slight incline from the barn.

Following, Taz studied the other outbuildings, the barn being the largest. He guessed that the long low building between the barn and the house was probably a bunkhouse. A tall shed stood behind that structure housing a collection of tractors and implements. "Do all the patients stay at the ranch house?" he asked.

"Not all of them. Some stay in the bunkhouse."

Damn. That could be a problem. If he stayed in the bunkhouse, how would he protect the therapist? "Shouldn't I be in the bunkhouse?"

"I don't have any bunks made up at this time. You'll have to stay at the main house."

"Where do you and Miss Kendricks live?"

"I have a separate room and bathroom at one end of the bunkhouse. Some of the kids we get need a little guidance to keep from breaking things."

"Breaking things?"

Blackstock snorted. "Mostly I'm there to keep them from breaking heads. Some of them harbor a lot of anger at their new lot in life. At times they take it out on each other."

Taz understood. He barely held his own anger in check. If he concentrated on little things, like the crunch of their boots on the gravel, he managed to calm himself.

"The house is fairly large, with seven bedrooms and three bathrooms. The ranch foreman has one of the rooms on the ground level. Miss Mize, one of the clients, and Miss Kendricks occupy two of the rooms upstairs. The ranch financial manager is only here once a month for two to three days at a time. He uses one of the other rooms, when he's here."

As they approached the back porch, Taz looked up at the two-story house. "Where do the owners stay?"

"Not here. But we keep the master suite available if they should ever decide to pay us a visit."

"How often do they come?"

"Since I've been here…never," Blackstock replied. "It's some kind of faceless investment group."

Taz didn't know what Blackstock was up to, but he suspected most, if not all, of the patients lived in the bunkhouse. Why would he insist on Taz taking a room in the main house? Not that he minded. Being in the main house gave him better access to Miss Kendricks at night. Being close would allow him to protect her better. For the sake of being under cover, though, he protested. "Look, I can stay in the bunkhouse with the others."

"No need. By the way, can you cook?"

"The extent of my culinary skills is slinging a steak on a grill. Why?"

"It's Cookie's night off. Which means you're cooking tonight in the big house. All new clients get a turn at KP duty—that's Kitchen Patrol. You're no exception. Remember that part about pulling your own weight?"

Taz nodded.

Blackstock led the way into the house and up a sweeping staircase

Taz absorbed as much of the layout and furnishings as he could, noting the large living area to the right and another hallway on the left side of the stairs.

On the upper floor landing, Blackstock stopped at the second door on the right. "You can dump your duffel bag here. The bathroom is across the hall. You share it with everyone on this end of the hallway. Be courteous and don't take long showers."

"No worries." He'd mastered short showers when he'd been in Afghanistan. They were lucky to get anything better than a trickle out of the portable showers the army erected. When they were on maneuvers, a spit bath with a moist towelette was the best he'd gotten.

"If you're done here, you might want to go help Hannah with the fence she's mending. She's out in the pasture behind the barn."

Taz walked down the steps in front of Blackstock. "I was told Miss Kendricks was a therapist. Why is she mending fences?" He stopped at the bottom and waited.

"Everyone pulls their weight around here, including Miss Kendricks." A small smile tilted Blackstock's mouth. "She leads by example. That woman doesn't know a task too hard. And she really cares about the ranch, the animals and the people here. Brighter Days Ranch is her home."

Taz frowned. "She doesn't own it, does she? I thought you said it was owned by an investment group."

Blackstock laughed. "Oh, Hannah wishes she owned the ranch." His laughter faded. "But, no, she doesn't. She grew up here. Her mother was the housekeeper."

Taz's mother had been the maid in the owner's house on the ranch where he'd grown up, too. His father had been one of the ranch hands who'd helped manage the five-thousand-acre spread in south Texas. Taz knew what being the poor ranch worker's kid was like. He'd worked hard to get off the ranch and to make a good living. "I take it she went away to college after high school?" Taz questioned as they passed through the house toward the kitchen and the back door.

"Hannah left the ranch for a while. Her mother insisted she go to college. Hannah agreed, with every intention of returning someday."

"Is her mother still the housekeeper?"

A shadow passed over Blackstock's face. "No, she died of a stroke the year Hannah graduated from college. She was a good woman. She never complained and worked hard so that Hannah wouldn't be in debt to student loans."

"You would think, once her mother died, she wouldn't want to come back to the ranch."

"And she wouldn't have, except the owner wanted to retire. He sold the ranch to an investment group which gave Hannah an offer she couldn't refuse." Blackstock pushed open the back door and held it for Taz to step out onto the porch before following him. "They asked her if she'd be interested in starting up a rehab facility for wounded warriors."

"Very noble of them."

"Hannah had resumes out to Walter Reed and other veteran rehab facilities." Blackstock dipped his chin. "Because of my injury, she wanted to do something for me and others in similar situations." He bent and tapped his right calf, making a hard metallic sound.

Taz had noticed the man's limp, but he hadn't suspected it was because he had a prosthetic device.

"When Hannah called to ask my advice and invited me to come work for the ranch, I was thrilled and grateful. Being here gave me a real purpose and a place to fit in. This area is my home. With only one leg, I wasn't sure how I'd get a job doing what I love best, taking care of horses." Blackstock ran a hand through his hair. "I don't know what or where I'd be now if not for the rehab ranch."

As he walked across the yard toward the barn, Taz searched for Hannah. "Have you met the people involved in the investment group?"

Blackstock shook his head. "No. I don't believe there's been a need for them to visit. Between Hannah and Percy, the foreman, they keep this place going. The horses and the people who come here to rehabilitate receive the best treatment they could possibly get. We have access to the local veterinarian and doctors. The investment group pays the bills."

Taz liked the concept, and would love to be involved in something as rewarding as helping injured service members and abused horses. "Sounds like a well-run facility. And the patients? Are they getting what they need?"

Blackstock grinned. "Don't let Hannah hear you call them patients. She insists they be termed clients. She doesn't want them leaning on their injuries or disabilities, thinking they are still in a medical environment. We don't take them on unless they are physically well. We're working on making them mentally well."

So far Taz understood Hannah and Percy's roles. He shot a glance toward Blackstock. "What are you in charge of?"

"I help the clients work with the horses we rehabilitate." Blackstock opened the gate to the pasture and paused. "Have you worked with horses much?"

Taz nodded. "I grew up on a ranch in south Texas. I know a few things about horses and cattle."

Blackstock grinned and pounded him on the back, giving him a little push through the open gate. "Great. You and Hannah will have a lot in common." He pointed. "She's at the far corner of the pasture. I believe she could use a hand stretching the wire."

With a nod, Taz left Blackstock and hurried across the field to where he could see Hannah bending close to a wooden fencepost. The pounding sound that echoed against the nearby hills indicated she was probably hammering nails into the post.

Taz glanced in all directions, aware of how exposed the woman was to anyone who wanted to target her. He didn't like that she was out in the field alone. From what Hank had told him, nobody had tried to shoot her. So far, the threats had been in a series of events that could be construed as accidents. A rail in the barn that had been intentionally loosened—the hammer's claw indention obvious in the wood. Hannah leaned on that rail every day when she helped fetch hay from the loft. Then the mishap occurred with the strap on her favorite saddle. Yes, the leather was old, but it hadn't broken. It had been severed by something sharp.

The final straw had been the tractor's tampered brakes. In the hills of Montana, brakes meant the difference between life and death. Hannah had been smart enough to bail from the tractor onto a tree branch. If she'd tried to throw herself from the seat onto the ground, she might not have jumped far enough to avoid the blades of the hay mower behind the tractor.

No, these were not accidents. Someone had it in for Hannah. And here she was, standing in the open, an easy target for someone with a half-decent knowledge of shooting a rifle with a scope. Picking up his pace, Taz was practically running by the time he reached her.

She straightened and lifted a hand to shield her eyes from the sun.

When he was close enough, he slowed to a walk, tamping down anger at her complete disregard for her own safety.

"Where's the fire?" she asked, dropping her hand. A scowl marred her pretty forehead. In blue jeans and the manure-stained blue chambray shirt, her hair pulled back in a ponytail, she wasn't the kind of beauty advertisers put on the glamour magazines.

She was the kind of woman who appealed to Taz. Gutsy, determined and sexy in an outdoorsy way. And the tool belt slung around the curve of her hips turned him on even more. "No fire," he said. "I thought you might need a hand stretching the wire."

Her eyes narrowed as if she were considering his words. Then she nodded toward the ground where a metal tool lay with a strand of barbed wire wrapped around a hook. "Ever handled a come-along?"

"I've stretched a few fences in my time."

"Good. Take it down to the next wooden brace post and tighten the strand. I'll hammer in the staples along the way."

Working together, they had the strand of barbed wire strung a hundred feet at five inches above the top of the welded-wire fence line. Repeating the task, they strung another row of barbed wire five inches above the last, matching the rest of the fence around the pasture.

When they'd finished, Hannah gathered her bucket of nails and strode across to where Taz wrapped the end of the barbed wire back around the staples she'd hammered into the end of the strand.

Lifting the roll of barbed wire, he asked, "What's next?"

"I need to ride the outer fences and see if any are down. We've had wolf attacks in the area, and I want to make sure the fences are up and discouraging them from coming after our weaker horses." She started back toward the barn. "You know your way around fences. Do you ride?"

Walking alongside her, he nodded. "Yes, ma'am."

"Good. And you don't have to call me ma'am. It makes me feel old."

"Yes, ma'am."

She glared at him.

The way her delicate brows descended and the flash in her blue eyes made tugged at something inside Taz. Why an angry female would make his chest tighten was beyond him. But he couldn't help it, and he laughed. Raising his hands, he smiled. "Sorry. I'll refrain from calling you ma'am. What would you prefer? Miss Kendricks?"

"Hannah." Color rose up in her cheeks. She ducked her head as she reached the barn. "You can ditch the barbed wire in the tack room. And ask Gavin to give you the shotgun and some shells. We might need protection if we run across a pack of wolves." She raised her brows. "You do know how to fire a gun, don't you?"

Taz fought back a grin. He could fire quite a number of weapons and was considered an expert marksman. "I used to hunt when I was a teen, and I've fired a weapon on numerous occasions."

"It's been a while since you were a teen." She tilted her head, studying him. "Sure you can handle a shotgun? They're different than the rifles you used in the military. The recoil is a bitch."

He nodded. "I'm sure."

For a moment, she continued to stare at him.

Taz didn't flinch. He liked that she was studying him. Her perusal gave him the excuse to study her in return.

Finally, she said, "I'll be saddling our horses when you're ready."

"Yes, ma—" He stopped himself short and continued, "Hannah." Then he winked.

Her cheeks reddened, and she swung away. "Don't be long."

Taz almost grinned at her discomfort. Who'd have thought a wink would make the tough-as-nails Hannah blush?

Hannah stepped into the pasture beside the barn and whistled for her horse. The buckskin gelding raced up to her, tossing his head, eager to see her. She reached into her pocket for the carrot she'd stuffed into it earlier that morning and snapped it in half.

"Hey, Frisco." She patted his nose and held out the piece of carrot.

The gelding nuzzled her palm for the carrot.

"Wanna go for a ride?"

Again, he tossed his head.

Hannah clipped the lead on his halter and led him into the barn. Once she had him tied to a metal ring, she went back out to get Little Joe, the bay gelding she used with all new clients. He had the gentlest nature and smoothest gait of all the riding horses on the ranch. Unsure of Taz's riding skills, she didn't want to risk putting him on the wrong animal.

As if he'd read her mind, Little Joe was waiting at the fence, ready for the other half of the carrot she'd given to Frisco.

When she led Little Joe into the barn, she stopped for a moment and stared at Taz, tossing a saddle over Frisco's back. He'd shed his button-down shirt when he'd been out stretching fence. Through the dark T-shirt he'd worn beneath it, his muscles bulged and flexed with each movement.

Hannah's breath caught in her throat, and she almost turned and ran back out to the pasture. How could she work with this man if all she could think of was touching those wonderfully broad shoulders?

She squared her own shoulders, reminding herself she was the therapist and he was the client. She had to act like a professional, not a lovesick teenager.

With her game-face on, she marched into the barn and tied Little Joe to a ring on the side of a post. "You'll ride Little Joe. The buckskin is mine."

"Blackstock let me know. And he finished the repairs on your saddle." He pulled the strap tight around Frisco's belly, secured it and dropped the stirrup in place. "Give me a minute and I'll have Little Joe saddled." He ran his hand along Frisco's neck and scratched behind the gelding's ears.

Frisco leaned his face into Taz's shoulder, nuzzling him.

Taz returned to the tack room.

Hannah watched until he disappeared through the door. Then she approached Frisco. "Traitor," she said, rubbing the animal's forehead. "See if I bring you another carrot."

Frisco tossed his head and nudged her pocket where she kept the treats. "Too late. You already burned that bridge."

Taz emerged carrying another saddle and blanket. He laid the blanket on Little Joe and settled the saddle over it, speaking softly to the animal as he reached beneath the gelding's belly for the girth.

Hannah checked his work on Frisco, noting he'd done everything perfectly. "Tell me a little about yourself, Mr. Davila."

"Taz," he insisted.

"Taz." She bet he was the devil in bed. Immediately, her cheeks burned and she ducked behind Frisco, praying the heat would dissipate before she had to face the new client again. Where were these thoughts coming from? They had to be due to her earlier conversation with Gavin. If he hadn't brought up her need to date, she wouldn't be having lusty thoughts about Taz.

Yeah, keep telling yourself that, and maybe you'll start believing it.

"I grew up in south Texas, on a ranch."

"So, this will be easy for you." Hannah left him adjusting the stirrups for his long legs and entered the tack room.

Gavin sat at the desk, grinning like a fool.

She glared. "Stop."

"I'll lay money on it that he's the one," Gavin said.

Her cheeks burning even hotter, Hannah shot a glance over her shoulder, praying Taz hadn't heard Gavin's remark. "He's *not* the one. I don't get involved with clients."

"Because you haven't met one you felt like getting involved with." Gavin tipped his head toward the door. "Until now."

"Not happening." She grabbed two bridles from nails on the wall. "So don't start planning the wedding."

Gavin stared up at the corner ceiling. "I'm thinking fall would be nice, with the foliage changing. You could have it at that pretty little church in Eagle Rock."

"Seriously, you'd think you were the girl, not me."

Shaking his head, Gavin snorted. "Sometimes I think you need a little more girl in your attitude. No wonder you haven't gotten laid in a very long time."

"Do you have a bridle—" a voice behind her started and stopped. "Sorry, I didn't mean to interrupt."

Hannah thought her head might spontaneously combust from the heat of her embarrassment. She spun, shoved the bridle in his hands and raced past him.

"Was it something I said?" Taz asked.

Gavin's chuckle made Hannah want to throw something at her friend, but she wouldn't go back into the tack room while Taz was there. She needed space away from the man who was making her insides mush.

Unfortunately, she wasn't getting the needed space. The dratted man followed her, carrying the bridle.

"Are you all right?"

"I'm fine. Why do you ask?" she said, sliding the bridle between Frisco's teeth, careful to avoid looking toward Taz.

"Your face is flushed. Are you sure you're not coming down with a fever, or maybe you got too much sun earlier?"

"I'm fine, damn it," she said through clenched teeth. "If you're ready, we should be on our way. The sun will set in a couple hours, and I want to cover as much ground as possible."

"Ready when you are," he said, leading Little Joe by the reins toward the barn door.

Grabbing Frisco's reins, she followed, her gaze on the thought-consuming man's backside. From behind, he was even more alluring. The way he swaggered when he walked, how straight he held his body and the sheer breadth of his shoulders pulled tight by the T-shirt he wore were enough to make her pant.

Her only saving grace was that she'd have to ride ahead of him since she knew where they were going. Then, at least, she wouldn't have to look at him.

But he'd be looking at her.

Ha! The man could have any female he wanted with only the crook of his finger. Why would he look twice at a woman who never wore makeup and rarely did anything more with her hair than pull it back in a ponytail?

She opened the gate, led her mount through and waited for Taz to walk by with Little Joe.

His lips twitched on the corners as he passed her.

Was he laughing at her? Anger replaced lust—okay, so it didn't *replace* the sensual reaction—but she latched onto it to keep from losing her cool. She shut the gate and mounted Frisco.

Taz slipped his foot into the stirrup and swung up into his saddle with the grace of a man who knew horses and riding like it was second nature.

Done with drooling, she nudged Frisco's flanks with her heels, sending him galloping across the field heading east into the hills. She leaned low over her horse's neck, letting him have his head. He loved racing and loved even more being first.

Hooves pounded the earth beside them as Little Joe caught up and kept pace with the buckskin.

As they neared a rise, Hannah slowed her horse. She couldn't outrun Taz, or the feelings she was experiencing about him. Taking those emotions out on the horses wasn't fair to Frisco and Little Joe.

The two mounts slowed to a walk, abreast of each other.

She might as well learn more about the new client, if she was going to be of any help to him. "Why didn't I know you were coming? Most of the time, we receive notice before the person shows up."

"It was a last-minute decision on my part," he answered, his cowboy hat shading his eyes.

"Still, I check my emails every morning before I head out."

"That's strange," he said. "You should have received word by yesterday, when I scheduled my flight."

"You were taking a chance by arriving without confirmation. What if we'd been full?"

He shrugged. "I figured I'd always wanted to visit Montana. If you didn't have room, I'd spend time exploring."

She rode along the fence line in silence for a little while, hoping the man would open up on his own and tell her why he was there. When he didn't, Hannah dove in. "I don't detect a limp, both of your arms are intact and you're riding that horse like you're physically capable of just about anything." Hannah leveled her gaze on him. "Why are you at this rehab facility?"

Instead of being intimidated by her straight question, he chuckled. "I was wondering when you'd ask."

His chuckle was warm, rich and intoxicating. The stiffness in Hannah's spine loosened, and she smiled. "And I was wondering when you'd tell."

His mouth straightened into a tight line. "I was medically discharged after suffering a TBI."

She shot a glance in his direction, studying his head. "Traumatic brain injury?"

"You'll not find any signs of the injury. I was involved in an explosion that basically rattled my brain. I spent the past three months relearning how to walk, dress myself and run. I guess I'm more fortunate than others. Once I started therapy, my memories came back pretty quickly. For the most part."

"What do you mean *for the most part?*"

For a long moment, he stared into the distance without replying. Then he looked toward her. "The muscle memory is back. But, I have difficulties controlling my anger, and I have situational memory loss."

"I thought those issues were what most men had troubles with," Hannah joked. When Taz didn't smile, she felt bad about her quip and forced a smile. "Sorry. I was just joking. You must have gone through a tough time. And look how far you've come. In three months, you've relearned so much."

"Yeah, but not what happened before the explosion, or why three of my men died and I didn't."

So, that was it. He had survivor's guilt.

"I keep thinking I missed something

important. If only I could remember what I saw, I might figure out the whole situation. Then my men wouldn't have died in vain."

"Perhaps you're trying too hard. Being here in the peace and quiet of the Montana countryside, working with the horses, might help you to relax and let your memories come back on their own."

Jaw tight, he looked away. "That's why I'm here."

"Good. A little hard work won't hurt you or your muscles. And, if I'm not mistaken, there's one of our charges now. She shouldn't be out this far when wolves are in the area." Hannah nudged Frisco's flanks, sending him at a trot in the direction of the rescued mare.

"She's one of our more recent residents. The poor creature was found on a small farm where the old gentleman who owned her couldn't feed her anymore. The county sheriff called the Brighter Days Rehab Ranch to help.

"Percy and I took the horse trailer to the old man's place on the far side of the neighboring county. She didn't even have the strength to resist. When we got her back to the ranch, she was lying in the bed of the trailer. We thought the trip had been too much on her.

"The vet came out and got her started on an IV, pumping nutrients into her body. It was touch-and-go through the night, but look how far she's come."

"She looks like a bag of bones," Taz

commented.

"True. She still needs to put on a little more weight. We keep her up around the barn so that we can feed her a lot more than she can get foraging on her own. Now that she has more energy, she finds ways to escape the corral. I bet Gavin doesn't know she's out."

As they trotted up to her, she skittered away a few feet.

"Ah, sweet Bella, it's okay. We just want to take you home to keep you safe. Come on, pretty girl," Hannah cooed. She dismounted her gelding, one hand outstretched.

Bella's ears flattened against her head and her eyes rolled back. She danced farther away, but didn't run. That was a good sign. A better reaction would be if she weren't afraid at all. The closer Hannah moved, the farther away the mare shifted.

Hannah backed up to where Taz stood beside his horse. "Perhaps we could herd her back to the barn."

"Let me try," he said.

She gestured toward the horse. "Go for it."

"Do you mind?" He held out the reins for Little Joe.

"Not at all." Hannah stood back with both horses and watched as the big former Army Ranger inched toward the mare, crooning to her in a deep, resonant tone. He spoke in Spanish, the words rolling off his tongue like music.

Hannah didn't think it possible, but the man

just got even sexier. She could imagine him speaking to her while they lay naked in bed, his fingers trailing across her body, followed by his lips and his words, warm against her skin.

Then he eased his hand up to the mare's halter, hooking his fingers in the nylon straps.

Bella reared, knocking Taz in the temple with her nose.

He swayed, but maintained his hold. When the mare finally settled down, Taz led her toward Hannah.

She snapped the spare lead rope she always carried onto the mare's halter. "That was amazing," she said, turning in time to see Taz drop to his knees.

Chapter 5

Gray fog crept in around Taz's vision as soon as the horse hit him in the side of the head. He held it together, his hand on the mare's halter holding him up more so than his own legs. Somehow he managed to lead the mare to where Hannah stood before the gray fog completely dimmed his vision.

His knees gave out and he slipped to the ground.

"Taz," a voice called out to him as if from the end of a long tunnel. "Taz, speak to me," the sweet voice commanded.

"I'm here," he answered. And the fog lifted, his vision cleared and he could control his muscles again. He glanced up into the beautiful blue eyes of an angel.

Her brows were pulled together in a deep frown and three horses looked over her shoulder as she knelt beside him.

"What's wrong?" he asked

She smiled, the frown lifting only slightly. "What's wrong?" Her gaze ran over him. "One minute you're handing me a horse, the next you're on your knees in the dirt. You tell me what's wrong and we'll handle it."

He wiped a hand down his face. "I guess you won't believe me if I said I was giving thanks for allowing me to snag the mare?"

Hannah shook her head and slipped her free hand under his arm. "Can you stand?"

"Sure." With heat burning up his neck into his cheeks, he rose to his feet in a hurry to get past the humiliation of passing out in front of the woman he was supposed to be protecting. Apparently he rose too quickly. That damned gray fog rushed in at the sides of his vision.

"Here, lean on me." Hannah draped his arm over her shoulder and wrapped hers around his waist. "If you feel yourself losing it, let me know. I can ease you to the ground. If you don't warn me, I'll cushion your fall. Because there's no way I can hold you up by myself."

As he listened to Hannah's calm voice, Taz's vision cleared, and he felt steadier on his feet. But he didn't want Hannah to let go. He liked how she fit beneath his arm. Despite her words to the contrary, he suspected she was strong enough to hold him up even if he should pass out. But he'd be damned if he would.

She felt firm but soft and feminine. The sun had reached its zenith hours before and had steadily fallen toward the horizon, taking its warmth with it. Hannah's body pressed against his side, warming him through her shirt and his. He didn't want to step away, but they had to get back to the house before dark, and they had a long way to go.

"Think you can ride without falling?"

"Yes," he answered, and prayed he'd spoken

the truth.

She stared up into his eyes, her brow furrowing. "I don't trust you to ride by yourself. You're riding with me. That way I can feel when you're slipping and keep you from falling to the ground."

He started to argue, his ego bruised as it was, but then he reminded himself that he'd have the advantage of being really close, if they rode together. And what better way to protect her than to envelop her body with his? "If you think that's best." He waved toward the horses. "You're the boss."

"Since Little Joe is the biggest horse, we'll ride him. Need help getting up?" she asked.

"I can do this." He stuck his foot in the stirrup and swung over the top. None of the gray fog returned and he didn't feel like it would. If he were a real gentleman, he'd tell her. Then again, he really liked the feel of her against him.

He kicked his boot free of the stirrup and started to slip over the back of the saddle.

"Oh, no you don't," Hannah said. "I'm riding in back in case you fall." She reached for the saddle horn, stuck her foot in the empty stirrup and tried to pull herself up.

She got halfway there, lost her grip and would have fallen if Taz hadn't grabbed her hand and pulled her up and across his lap.

Hannah landed hard against his chest.

Taz wrapped his arms around her to steady her. "It's a good thing I like the rich, earthy smell of horse manure." He grinned.

"I'm supposed to be helping you, not the other way around. Some therapist I am." Hannah tried to straighten.

All her wiggling had a marked effect on Taz's libido. "Hey, be still for a minute, or we'll both end up on the ground."

Thankfully, Little Joe was patient and stood quietly as Taz and Hannah moved about in the saddle.

"Since you're already in front of me, you might as well stay there. I promise, if I start to fall, I'll let you hold onto my arms to keep me up." He stared into those startlingly blue eyes and felt his jeans tightening. "Agreed?"

She held his gaze for a long moment and her tongue snaked out to wet her lips. "Agreed." Hannah maneuvered her leg over the saddle horn, still sitting in his lap. She lifted the reins in her capable hands and leaned out to snag Bella's lead and Frisco's reins.

"I can take those."

"Are you sure?"

"I'll hold them and wrap my arms around your waist. Will that make you feel better?"

"Yes," she said, her voice a little breathy. "Of course."

The irony of the situation didn't escape Taz. The rehab client held the bodyguard client around the waist all the way back to the ranch.

"Are you sure you're okay the way you are?" she asked, several times.

Hell no, he wasn't. Every time the horse swayed, Hannah's bottom ground against his crotch, stirring up a desire so strong, he could barely breathe.

He promised himself a really long, cold shower when he got back to the main house. Even then, he'd probably end up with the worst case of blue balls he'd ever imagined. And, he didn't see any sign of relief in the near future. This might be the toughest assignment yet.

"So, you grew up on a ranch in south Texas?"

He nodded, and then realized she couldn't see the movement. "Yes," he said, trying not to sound like he was in physical pain, but not up to a long conversation.

"You worked with horses and cattle?"

"Yes. And big game."

"Really? Like what?"

"White tail, elk, axis, fallow and red deer and wild boar."

"Aren't wild boar dangerous?" Hannah shifted, her bottom grinding against his growing erection.

Taz bit down on his tongue to keep from groaning.

She shifted again

The pain eased, and he unclenched his jaw. "Yes, a wild boar can kill you. I once saw a man gored so badly he spent the next month in ICU."

That man had been goaded by his friends to go boar hunting with nothing but a knife. Even as a teenager, Taz tended to believe in Darwin's theory of survival of the fittest. Fortunately for the owner of the game ranch, the man survived. Taz bet he wasn't friends anymore with the men who'd dared him. If he was, he deserved them.

"Did your family own the ranch?"

"No, my mother and father worked on the Triple Diamond Ranch. I had the benefit of living there through my childhood."

"And you joined the army straight out of high school?"

"Yes," he said.

"Isn't it hard to get into the Army Rangers?" she asked.

"Can be." For him, making it through Ranger training was a test of his courage and abilities. He liked to push himself and going through Ranger training had done that.

Putting that training to use on the battlefield was yet another challenge he'd undertaken with pride and determination. Perhaps his pride had been the chief factor in his final battle. If he hadn't been so full of his ability, he wouldn't have been injured, and the other three members of his team would still be alive.

"What were their names?"

"Whose?" he asked, his arms tightening around her middle.

"The men who died in the explosion," she said, her voice soft, undemanding. "You don't have to talk about it if you don't want to."

He didn't want to. Not when he was in pain

from her bottom rubbing against his dick. But her tone had opened up something he'd locked down three months ago when he'd awakened up in the hospital in Landstuhl.

He swallowed hard against the lump in his throat. "Ryan Guthrie, Jason Klingensmith and Theo McCormick."

"Did they leave behind family?" she persisted.

Again, he swallowed to clear the knot choking his vocal cords. "Ryan left behind a wife. Thankfully no children. But he was an only child. His parents took his death hard."

Hannah rested a hand on his and gave it a gentle squeeze. "Losing someone you love is something you never get over."

Taz agreed. He'd loved his teammates like brothers. They'd forged a bond through danger and hard times. Each was willing to give his life for the others. And they had. "Klingensmith had a wife and two little girls. They'll never know what a great man their father was."

Hannah's hand tightened on his. "I know how hard that can be. I didn't know my father."

"Divorce?"

She shook her head. "He was never in the picture. My mother never mentioned him or told me his name. I figure it didn't matter. If he didn't want to stick around to be a part of my life, I didn't want anything to do with him either." She laughed, the sound completely without humor. "I did fine without him. I grew up on this ranch, surrounded by quite a few men who filled in for the missing father figure."

Taz could hear the pride in her voice and also the sadness for something that would never be.

Though they'd both grown up on a ranch, that's where their common ground ended. Where Hannah had been raised by a single mother, Taz had been one of three children raised by two hardworking parents who'd loved their children dearly.

"What about McCormick?" Hannah asked.

Her question puled him away from his poor, but happy, childhood and back into the deep sadness war had created. "He was supposed to get married when we got back from deployment. His fiancée wanted to push the wedding forward and get married before he left. He thought doing so would jinx the mission. He said having her waiting for him when he got back would give him even more reason to make it back alive."

Taz's throat closed off on the last word. When McC didn't make it back, his fiancée had been devastated. "She committed suicide when she heard of his death."

"Oh, sweet Jesus," Hannah exclaimed. "I'm so sorry for the loss of all of them."

"Yeah. Me, too."

Taz inhaled the earthy scent of her hair, wishing he could join her in the shower she'd take when they returned to the house. Maybe, if he lost himself in her, for a moment he could forget the faces of his brothers-in-arms and the people they'd left behind. None of them should have died. Deep down, he knew something had gone terribly wrong, and he was the key to figuring out what that something was. If only he could remember.

The anger surged inside him, pounding his blood against his eardrums. His body stiffened. If he couldn't find some way to release the tension, he'd explode into a million pieces.

"Uh, Taz?" Hannah said quietly.

Through the blinding rage whirling around him like a cyclone, he heard her voice.

"Taz," she said, her tone more urgent.

"What?" he snapped out.

"Loosen up, will ya?" She tugged at his arms. "You're hurting me."

Immediately, he dropped his arms from around her waist and leaned back, huffing out a breath. "I'm sorry."

"Don't be. It was my fault. I poked at a sore spot. It was bound to happen." She wrapped one arm around her middle.

"Are you all right?" he asked, afraid to touch her. Afraid he'd hurt her again.

"I'm fine. I was just having a hard time breathing." She glanced over her shoulder and frowned. "Really, I'm fine." With her free hand, she pulled his arms back around her waist. "Now hold on. I can't have you toppling off Little Joe. He's the biggest horse we have and a fall from him is bound to cause some damage."

If he could have gotten off the horse without

dislodging Hannah, Taz would have. God, what was wrong with him? Had the TBI made him lose his effing mind? Never in his life had he hurt a woman. Until now.

As soon as he could, he'd tell Patterson he wasn't fit for duty. The army had been right to discharge him. Had he gone back to active duty, he'd have been a menace to his comrades, and posed a danger to society. Once again, he wondered why he'd been spared. He and everyone around him would be better off if he'd died in that explosion.

Hannah reined Little Joe to a halt and twisted in Taz's lap until she faced him. She raised a hand to his cheek and forced him to look at her. "Hey, you big dumbass. You didn't hurt me. I can tell by your body language that you're beating yourself to death."

She tapped his cheek lightly.

Not enough to hurt him, but enough to get across her message. His narrowed his eyes.

"You didn't hurt me." She said, "I'm fine. You have to believe you're alive for a reason. If you die, your buddies will have given *their* lives in vain. You're responsible for living your life to the fullest. If not for you, then do it for them." She leaned closer until her nose touched his. "They would have done the same."

After her rant ceased, all Taz could think about was how lush her lips were and how much he wanted to kiss them.

"Do you hear me?" she asked, her brows

dipping deep.

His lips twitched. "Yes, ma'am."

"And don't call me ma'am. It makes me feel o—"

Before he could think of all the reasons he shouldn't, Taz claimed her lips. And they were every bit as lush and soft as he'd imagined.

At first, she stiffened. Within seconds, her body melted against his.

For such a tough woman with the heart of a lion, she was all soft and pliant in his arms.

She let out a breath on a gasp, her lips and teeth parting just enough.

Taz thrust inside, sliding his tongue along hers, tasting her sweetness.

Hannah ran her hands up his chest and feathered her fingers in his hair, dragging him closer.

He circled her waist, bringing her body flush with his. His erection grew harder, the discomfort at once painful and intoxicating.

Hannah returned the kiss, pressing her breasts against his chest, twisting her tongue around his.

Taz could have kissed her until the cows came home, but a tug on the reins and lead rope pulled him back to the reality with a jolt. He lifted his head and shot a glance toward the two horses in tow.

Bella whickered and tossed her head. Frisco danced beside her, pawing the ground impatiently.

Taz lifted his head and looked around.

Hannah's eyes rounded, and she pressed her fingers to her lips. "Sweet Jesus. That shouldn't have happened."

"But it did. I have no regrets."

"Oh, dear." She bit her lip, her brows descending. "This can't be. Kissing you breaks all the rules."

Taz shrugged. "Some rules were meant to be broken."

"Not these." She twisted back around and wiggled her way out of the saddle, dropping to the ground. "I think you're well enough to ride the rest of the way on your own. Let me know if you start getting dizzy. We can stop."

"I'm fine," he insisted. He'd rather she continued to ride with him. He liked the way she fit against him. And he could protect her better with his body wrapped around hers.

Based on the landmarks he'd observed on the way out, Taz figured they were near the ranch buildings. He suspected over the next hill he'd see the house and barn. And, in turn, the clients and workers would see them, too.

Taz understood Hannah's need to keep their kiss a secret from the others. She probably had established rules about keeping herself romantically apart from her clients. Revealing their clandestine kiss might destroy the image she'd been so determined to project.

But the need to be near enough to protect her made him follow her closely, his gaze panning the woods and fields, searching for a threat. Not that he'd run into any thus far. He was beginning to think the threat was to his own psyche. The more he was around the sexy therapist, the more he wanted to be.

Chapter 6

Hannah remained rigid in her saddle, cursing herself all the way back to the barn. What was she thinking by making out with a client? That one kiss was against every rule she'd ever thought up for her work at the ranch. She'd completely crossed the line.

And now that she had, she suspected she'd have a hard time forgetting how wonderful his mouth felt, his tongue caressing the length of hers. Not only did she enjoy the kiss, she wanted to do it again. And again. And again! What was worse...she didn't want to stop at just a kiss.

As they rode into the barnyard, Percy stepped out of the barn and took charge of Bella. "Everything all right?" he asked, staring from Hannah to Taz and back.

Hannah forced a small smile and slipped out of her saddle. "Perfectly all right." No, they weren't, but she didn't want to discuss her raging desires with the man who'd been more of a father to her as she was growing up. Talking about sex had been one of those subjects he'd conveniently avoided, and Hannah wouldn't have had it any other way. The man turned a startling shade of red, bordering on purple, when anything remotely referencing intercourse was discussed in mixed company.

84

"You gonna introduce me to your friend?" Percy asked.

"Oh, I'm sorry." Hannah's cheeks burned as she turned toward Taz. "Percy, this is our newest client, Alex Davila. He goes by Taz." Facing the older man, she continued, "Taz, this is Percy Pearson, the Brighter Days foreman."

The foreman reached up to shake Taz's hand "Nice to meet you, Taz. Gavin tells me you have KP duty tonight, as part of the Brighter Days initiation."

Taz nodded, his gaze on Hannah. "I do. But to give you fair warning, I'm not much good in the kitchen."

"That's fine. Gavin tells me you can grill. That'll do. The boys love a good steak every once in a while."

Taz nodded and swung down from his saddle.

His movements were fluid and sexy, his jeans fitting him snugly at the hips.

He passed Hannah, leading Little Joe into the barn.

She swallowed hard to keep from moaning at the flawlessness of the man's butt. Up until that moment, she'd considered herself a woman obsessed with a man's eyes. She had to re-evaluate her conviction. Taz's ass was perfection in motion, sensual and captivating.

Percy leaned close to her ear. "A girl has to be a little less obvious if she wants to get a man."

Hannah's jaw dropped, and she turned

toward the foreman. "What did you say?" Heat seared a path up her neck and into her cheeks.

"You have to play a little hard to get, not drool over his every move." He snorted. "I'm not blind. And neither is our new client."

Hannah squared her shoulders and tipped up her chin. "I'm not interested in Mr. Davila." She said it with the appropriate amount of conviction and almost could have believed it herself…if she hadn't kissed the man like it might be her last kiss on Earth.

"Amateur." Percy shook his head. "Didn't you learn to flirt in high school?"

"I most certainly did not. I was busy helping out on the ranch."

Percy crossed his arms over his chest and ran his gaze over her. "Gavin's right. We need to stage an intervention to get you on the right path to finding a man."

"What?" she said, aghast at what her shy, easily embarrassed, father figure had just admitted. "You and Gavin have been talking about me behind my back?"

Percy shrugged. "Nothing we wouldn't say to your face. You need to start looking for someone to share your life with. You don't want to end up like me, alone in your old age."

"You're not old. And it's not too late for you to find someone to be with. Women around your age would snap you up like a cat going after catnip."

"I don't reckon I want to be considered

catnip. Can't hardly stand cats. Except maybe that old tabby that keeps the mouse population from exploding in the barn." He waved his hand. "But that's beside the point. We were talking about you, not me."

"Oh, no, we weren't. My love life is off limits for the two of you." She rolled her eyes. "I can't believe you two were matchmaking. You're like a couple of old ladies."

"Hey, watch your mouth, young lady. Name-calling isn't sexy."

"And you know what sexy is?" She stormed past him. "Thanks, but no thanks. I told Gavin, I can manage on my own."

"Uh-huh. And when was your last date?"

"None of your business. It's not yours or Gavin's responsibility or right to dictate who I should go out with or how I should conduct myself."

Percy held up his hands. "Okay, okay. Don't get your panties in a twist. Just saying, you have to play a little hard to get, or you'll have the fella running the opposite direction."

"Oh, sweet Jesus," she muttered. Hannah entered the barn's shadowy interior and tied Frisco to a ring on a post.

Taz emerged from the tack room, carrying a currycomb and brush.

Little Joe stood patiently, stripped of his saddle blanket and bridle.

After setting the brush and currycomb on a ledge, Taz rounded Frisco, nudged Hannah out of the way and slung the stirrup up over the horse's back.

"Hey, don't get pushy with me." Anger replaced Hannah's earlier embarrassment. She didn't like it when men assumed that just because she was female, she couldn't pull her own weight. "I can do that myself."

"I know." His actions didn't slow one bit.

"Then move aside and let me."

"My mama taught me to be nice to women." He slipped the strap out of the girth and hauled the saddle and blanket off the horse. "I'll let you get the bridle."

Her lips pressed into a thin line, and she said in her most intimidating voice, "Don't patronize me." The fool had the nerve to grin.

"Anyone ever tell you that your eyes sparkle when you're mad?" He sailed past her into the tack room.

"I'm glad *someone* told her," Gavin called out. "She thinks she's one of the guys."

"As far as it goes around here," she called out, "I *am* one of the guys."

"Not from where I'm standing," a deep voice said behind her.

Hannah spun, her face flaming.

Franklin stood beside Vasquez, each with one hand on the wheelbarrow they'd pushed through the barn door. In the wheelbarrow was another one of the ranch's clients, Jimmy Young, a man who'd lost both legs but had full use of his arms. The man could get around almost as well as any of the two-legged people.

Franklin grinned. "I think Miss Kendricks is too pretty to hide away in the backwoods of Montana."

Vasquez nodded. "Finally, we've found something we can all agree on." He let go of his handle and held up his hand.

Franklin gave him a high-five.

Young took his turn slapping palms.

Hannah rolled her eyes. "You shouldn't be discussing me."

"You're the only female around, besides Mize," Young said.

Vasquez snorted. "She threatened to cut off our balls if we so much as made a pass at her."

"Damn right, I will." The woman in question limped into the barn, carrying a small ball of fur. Her focus shot to Hannah, her brows making a V over the bridge of her nose. "Doc, we've got a problem."

"What's wrong?" Hannah slung the bridle over a hook on the wall and hurried over to Lori. "And don't call me Doc. I'm not a doctor."

"You're the closest thing to a doctor we have out here and we could use one about now. Check out this little guy." She held out her hands.

"What have you got there?" Hannah stared down at the wiggling creature in her hands.

"Sydney had her puppies and she pushed this one out of the bed. He's the runt of the litter. I was afraid if I left him there, Sydney would eat him."

Franklin, Vasquez and Young laughed.

Lori gave them a killer glare. "Dogs sometimes eat their young if they don't think they're viable. Or if they just don't know what to do with them."

They snickered.

"Oh, grow up. You can look it up on the Internet." She turned back to Hannah. "Can we do anything for him? If we don't, he'll die for sure."

Hannah ran a finger over the puppy's warm body. "He'll need milk and feeding every two hours through the night. I can get in touch with the veterinarian and ask what he recommends.

"Anything." Lori's eyes filled with tears. "Just don't let him die."

Hannah stared down at the tiny blob of an Australian shepherd puppy speckled in black and gray spots. His eyes were closed tight, and he lay barely moving in Lori's palm.

Knowing Lori's history, Hannah understood what this defenseless little being meant to the woman. The woman's deployment to Afghanistan had ended tragically. Lori still experienced nightmares about the event and had difficulty sleeping.

Hannah had to do everything in her power to save that puppy. "Let's see what Mr. Blackstock has in the tack room. We'll need either a syringe or a tiny baby bottle. I know we don't have the bottle, but perhaps we can improvise. You carry him, he seems happy in your warm hands.

Besides, I'm filthy."

"Thank you, Hannah." A tear slipped from the corner of Lori's eyes. "He didn't have a chance with his mama."

Hannah's heart squeezed. "But you're giving him one. We'll do our best to keep him alive through the night. Tomorrow we can send someone into town for supplies."

"I'll stay up with him. All night, if I have to."

"We can take turns. No use you staying up so long."

"I don't mind. I just don't want the puppy to die."

Hannah nodded. "We'll do the best we can." She glanced over Lori's shoulder at Taz.

He met her gaze with a steady one of his own. Taz knew. The man had grown up on a ranch. Sometimes baby animals didn't make it, no matter how much effort you put into saving them. But they wouldn't know if they didn't try.

Gavin emerged from the tack room with a plastic syringe. "Here, you can use this to feed the pup. But I suggest you try to get him back with the bitch first."

"I tried," Lori insisted. "She wanted nothing to do with him and even snapped at him, like she might kill the poor thing. That's when I took him out."

"Then we'll have to take care of him until he's strong enough. Maybe then the mother will accept him back in the litter." Hannah looked around the barn. "What should we feed him tonight?"

Gavin appeared in the doorway of the tack room. "It's not good, but when it's the only thing you have, give him some goat's milk. First thing in the morning, you need to get dog milk replacement formula and probiotics. The puppy isn't getting the colostrum containing all the good stuff that protects him from germs and bacteria."

"We will." Lori nodded. "First thing."

"Look…" Gavin ran a hand through his hair. "I'll give the vet a call tonight. He might make an exception for us." He shook his head. "All this for a mutt. You women kill me."

Hannah gave her friend a twisted smile. "Yeah, like you wouldn't move mountains to save the little guy, too. You're nothing but a big softy, Gavin Blackstock. You can't tell me differently. I grew up with you."

"Whatever." He pointed at Lori. "Keep him warm while I make that call."

"Take him up to the house and get him a blanket," Hannah said. "I'll be right up after I tackle the goat for a little milk."

"I can do that," Lori offered.

"Let us help," Franklin said.

Vasquez nudged him in the gut. "What do we know about milking a goat?"

Franklin shrugged. "Nothing, but it doesn't hurt to learn."

"I'll give it a go." Jimmy said. "Dump me out of this thing, will ya?"

Vasquez and Franklin upended the

wheelbarrow, and Jimmy leveraged himself out onto the ground.

Hannah pointed at the two one-armed heroes. "You two take care of the horses. Lori, take the pup to the house. Taz, I'll need you to hold the goat while I milk her, and Young, you can learn by watching me. I'll even give you a crack at it."

Like the good soldiers they were, each of her clients snapped to attention and hurried to carry out her orders.

Hannah felt comfortable that Franklin and Vasquez could manage the three horses under Percy's guidance.

She motioned to Young and Taz. "Come on. We have a goat to milk, and I warn you. Lolita resists this procedure." The last time she'd tried to milk the old goat, she'd been butted, kicked and almost speared by one of the animal's killer horns.

Taz had proven handy with the spooked mare. How would he do with a cantankerous goat?

One thing was for sure…she wouldn't be as absorbed by her new client's presence while trying to squeeze a few drops of milk out of Lolita.

Young propelled his body by using his arms to lift his torso and hips. He wore thick leather gloves and heavy denim jeans with the legs cut out and the seat folded and sewn up. Despite the lack of legs, he moved quickly.

When he'd first arrived at the ranch, Hannah hadn't been certain what he could do to help out.

But Young had shown an exceptional connection with the horses. Gavin had built him a platform he could pull himself up onto in order to be closer to the horses' heads. He worked with Gavin to calm the abused animals. He cleaned and brushed them, talking softly just like Gavin had shown him.

Not only had the horses responded, they helped Young beat a depression that was even more debilitating than his lack of limbs.

Hannah snagged a clean milk pail from the tack room and hurried toward the barn's back exit.

Lolita stood in the field of the rear entrance to the barn, munching on feed someone had poured into her trough. Her two kids romped around her legs, hopping up onto the edge of the trough and down again, never slowing. They were in constant motion and a joy to watch, never failing to lift the lowest spirits.

When Lolita saw the three humans approaching she swung her hindquarters away, but continued eating from the trough.

Hannah cast a sideways glance at Taz. "If you could hold her head, Young and I will work on getting some of that milk."

Taz scooped a handful of feed from the trough and held it out to Lolita.

She chewed the feed in her mouth, eyeing Taz. When she'd finished the feed, she stretched out her neck and snuffled Taz's hand. He let her have a nibble, but held back a little, crooning nonsense as he crouched close to her.

Her kids—one black, the other spotted black and white—crowded around her, inching toward Taz. Eventually, one jumped up onto Taz's bent knee and then back down again.

Lolita took that moment to reach out again, trying to snag the remaining feed from Taz's hand.

He let her and then he scratched her forehead.

She butted his hand gently, as if encouraging him to keep scratching.

Taz did, running his hand up and down from her nose to the base of her horns. Then he wrapped a hand around her horn, braced himself and held on.

Once Lolita figured out she'd been caught, she backed up, bleating loudly. She kicked and twisted, but Taz didn't release his hold on the horn.

Instead, he talked to her in that same rich timbre that made Hannah's knees wobble.

Lolita settled, and her kids rushed toward her, rooting against her full udders, drinking their fill.

"Now's your opportunity," Taz said. "Come from behind and don't make any noise with that pail." His words were in the same tone he'd used to calm the beast.

Amazed at his ability to tame an ornery creature, Hannah did as he suggested and moved toward her from behind, slipping her pail beneath the neck of one of the kids and gently squeezing an udder, aiming a warm stream of milk into the tin bucket.

Young eased up next to Hannah.

"Your turn," she whispered. She showed him the motion she used to milk the goat, circling her fingers high on the long, tapering teat, and then demonstrated.

He watched closely and tried. At first, nothing came out. Young tried again and a stream squirted into the pail. He grinned at Hannah and continued until they had enough milk to feed an entire litter of puppies.

Hannah tapped Young's shoulder and backed away from the goat.

Young handed her the pail and moved to a position beside her, allowing the kids to complete their feeding uninterrupted.

Taz released Lolita's horn, still crooning softly.

She stepped back, but didn't run away.

"Well, that was a lot easier than I thought it would be." Hannah had to give credit where it was due. "You've got wonderful skills with the animals Taz. You'll fit in just fine on the ranch." Then she dragged her gaze away from Taz and smiled at Young. "Just so you know, not everyone gets milk on their first milking attempt. Well done."

Young beamed. "Thanks. Now, if you're done with me, I'd like to get cleaned up before chow."

"Speaking of chow…" Hannah raised her gaze to Taz. "I know a puppy who will be happy for anything, even goat's milk."

"And I'm on for grilling steaks," Taz said.

"You'd better get started, or you'll have a mutiny on your hands. These guys are a tough crowd when you don't deliver their meal on time." Hannah waved him toward the house. "Go on. I'll finish with the others and be up to help you as soon as they're done."

"I'd rather you showed me where everything is. It could take a lot longer to figure it all out, otherwise." He nodded toward Young. "Besides, I think the guys have everything under control and you have a starving puppy to feed."

"He's right." Gavin poked his head out of the barn. "I couldn't get hold of Dr. Waters. I left a message. If he doesn't return my call, I'll run into town first thing in the morning and get that formula and whatever else he says you need." He grinned at Hannah. "Get Lolita's milk to Lori. She needs it as much as the puppy."

Gavin was right. Then why was Hannah so hesitant to be alone with Taz again?

Because she wanted to be alone with him and wanted to run her hands and tongue all over his body. Hannah stumbled at the thought.

Taz hooked her elbow. "Steady there."

Steady? How could she be when all he had to do was talk to her in that deep, rich voice? And his touch sent sparks ripping through her, igniting a flame she had no idea how to control.

What did most women do in a situation like this? For the first time in her life, Hannah wished she'd paid more attention to the girly-girls in high school and college. Now she was completely out of her league with an alpha male, and her bodily reactions had her as jittery as a cat in a room full of rocking chairs.

Chapter 7

Taz could sense her hesitation to be alone with him. Her reticence was his fault. He'd kissed his client and changed the rules of the game. For her, as well as him.

Now she was so jumpy, she was like a new colt at his first time in a lunging ring. Was she afraid he'd kiss her again?

His groin tightened at the other possibility.

Was she afraid he wouldn't kiss her again?

Oh, he wanted to. Really bad. But doing so was wrong. He was supposed to be protecting her and looking around to determine who was responsible for the attacks on her person. Then he would neutralize the bastard. He scanned the area, searching the shadows. Nothing moved. Everyone was either in the barn taking care of the animals, or at the house getting ready for dinner.

Hannah was good, kind-hearted but tough as nails when it came to the wellbeing of her wounded warriors and rescue horses. She wanted the best for them, and sometimes, tough love was best.

He'd witnessed her tough love by the way she'd handled the fight between Vasquez and Franklin in the stalls earlier that day. She'd shown them what their shit-slinging had accomplished. And they all seemed to respect her for the way she didn't baby them.

Taz had a lot of respect for the men and women recuperating at the ranch. They'd have a tough road ahead of them with PTSD, on top of missing limbs. "What's Miss Mize's story?" he asked to take his mind off the woman beside him.

Hannah carried the pail of goat's milk, her gaze on the house. "She was on a convoy in Afghanistan when her vehicle hit an IED. Even though her leg was badly injured, she dragged herself over to her driving partner and held him in her arms as he bled out. I think she blames herself for letting him die."

"IED explosions are extremely destructive. You can't save everyone involved."

"No, but when you're the only one to survive, the guilt can be crippling."

Taz's lips tightened. That comment hit entirely too close to home. "Are you a physical therapist or a counselor?"

Hannah gave him a sideways glance. "Actually, I'm licensed in both. I thought the combination would be a good for what we're trying to accomplish here."

"Well, you don't have to try that pyscho-babble on me. I just need to remember what happened. What I might have seen on that mission could still help."

"Ever thought why you might not *want* to remember?"

The therapist tone in her voice made him stiffen. "I didn't watch my buddies die. I was out cold. I had no choice in whether or not they would have lived. I didn't even come to until I landed at the hospital in Landstuhl, Germany."

"Does that time-lapse bother you?" she asked.

"Stop," he said through gritted teeth. He'd been through countless sessions with a psychiatrist at Walter Reed. "I don't want you digging into my brain. I've had the mandated therapy. The doc signed off. I'm fine."

"Except when you pass out catching a horse." She stopped before she reached the house and put out a hand to stop him, too. "A TBI means you've had severe brain trauma. You can't expect to get back to normal on your own schedule. Recovery doesn't work that way."

"No shit. That's why I'm here."

Hannah raised her free hand to cup his cheek. "Maybe you need to find a new sense of *normal*. And I'm here to help. But you have to let me."

The familiar anger roiled in Taz's gut. He wanted to grab her and shake her. She didn't understand the feeling of utter futility he experienced every day. His three men died, and he didn't have any recollection of that day. Deep in his heart, he knew there was something he needed to remember about that mission. Something significant.

But he wasn't in Montana at the Brighter Days Rehab Ranch to be psychoanalyzed. He was supposed to be protecting this woman. From whom, he still didn't know. He'd do his best to figure it out, and soon. Again, he scanned the barnyard and the shadows surrounding the outbuildings. Was Hannah's tormentor nearby, watching and waiting for another opportunity to terrorize the pretty therapist?

Taz's fists clenched, frustration eating an ulcer into his belly. Like his memory, the person behind the attacks remained just out of reach.

They entered through the back door, leading into a mudroom. Hannah stomped her boots and then toed them off. "You don't need to remove your boots since you'll be going in and out to the grill with our supper." She grinned. "I like my steak medium."

He popped a salute. "Yes, ma'am."

Her grin slipped into a frown. "I told you, ma'am makes me feel old."

"Right." He touched two fingers to the corner of his brow in a mock salute. "Miss Kendricks."

Her frown deepened for a moment and then lightened. "I guess that will do. We need to keep us on a professional basis."

He slipped a hand around the back of her neck and tipped her head up, lowering his mouth to within a breath of hers. "Are you sure?"

She rested her free hand on his chest, her fingers curling into his shirt. "Yes," she said, the word nothing more than a faint whisper.

As much as he wanted to kiss her, he knew he couldn't. Then why was he holding her so close, teetering on the edge of doing just that?

Oh, what the hell.

He touched her lips in the briefest of kisses, skimming across their softness. He wanted so much more.

Footsteps inside the house awakened him to the fact they were no longer alone.

Taz stepped back, opened the door and held it for Hannah.

She took a deep breath, pasted a smile on her face and carried the pail of goat's milk into the kitchen where Lori stood holding the puppy, her face creased with worry.

"Oh, thank God. I think he's starving." She stroked the puppy, snuggled to her chest. "He's rooting around for something to eat, and I didn't know what else to do."

"We'll give him a little of the goat's milk to fill his belly, until we can get him onto replacement formula. His little tummy won't respond well to anything else."

"At least he won't have to go all night without some nourishment." Lori dragged in a shaky breath. "Thank you."

"I'll strain the milk. Then we can feed him with the syringe." Hannah moved to the sink, pulled out a glass, placed a thin, clean cloth over the rim and poured the goat milk onto the cloth. When the glass was full, she removed the cloth and filled the syringe. "Here you go. Mark the time. He'll need to be fed at least every two hours in the beginning."

Lori pressed the syringe into the puppy's mouth.

He rooted, pushing it aside.

Seeing her frustration, Taz took the syringe from her hand. "Here, let me help." He gently gripped the puppy's head, fit his thumb and finger into the sides of his mouth, pressing just hard enough to open it, stuck the tube down his throat and squirted goat milk a little at a time.

The puppy closed his mouth around the syringe and sucked.

"I think he has the idea now." Taz handed over the syringe.

Lori took the puppy into the living room to feed him more.

Hannah stood beside Taz, her lips curled in a smile. "Who knew Army Rangers could be so gentle?"

"Hey, we're only badass when we need to be." He nodded. "Now, show me some steaks. I have some rough and tough grilling to do before the occupants of the ranch stage a mutiny."

"Mixing army and navy, now?"

"We're all on this ship together. We either sink as one or swim as one." He shook his head. "Just show me the damned steaks."

Hannah chuckled, the sound warming Taz through to the core.

He touched her cheek. "You need to laugh more often. It suits you."

"We all could use a little more laughter." She walked to one of the industrial-sized refrigerators.

She pulled out several butcher paper-wrapped packages. "Laugh all you want, but don't burn my steak."

"Yes, m—"

Narrowing her gaze, she held up her hand. "Don't do it."

He laughed. "Yes, Hannah."

Her gaze shot up to his and held.

If he were a gambling man, he'd bet she liked the sound of her name on his lips. Good thing he didn't gamble. Thankfully, he had a little self-control at that moment, because he wanted to take her mouth in a soul-searing kiss.

She shoved the packages of meat into his hands. "You cook. I'm showering the stench off of me."

"Good. I was beginning to think you liked smelling like the back end of a horse." Gavin stepped into the kitchen, a grin spreading across his face. He tipped his head toward the stairs. "Go. I'll show Taz where he can find the grill and charcoal. There's a bunch of starving people counting on him to get this, the most important mission of the day, right."

Hannah headed for the staircase.

Taz's gaze followed her until she disappeared.

"She's a ball-buster, that girl," Gavin commented, his gaze on Hannah, as well. "She'll make someone a helluva partner. I have to admit, I measure every woman I date against her, and they all seem to come up short. But she's right, we love each other, but there's no chemistry." He shrugged and turned to pin Taz with a meaningful stare. "Not like the chemistry I can already see between you and her."

Taz frowned. He wasn't supposed to have anything with Hannah. And Blackstock sure as hell shouldn't notice chemistry between Taz and Hannah. "I don't know what you're talking about."

"Yeah, keep deluding yourself." He turned toward the door. "I'm closer to Hannah than anyone, besides Percy and I can tell you're melting her butter. Come on, we have steaks to cook."

Taz shot one last glance toward the staircase. Yes, something was stirring between him and Hannah, but he didn't realize the emotion was so obvious. He'd have to tone it down, or he'd lose focus on his mission. And he couldn't afford to lose focus. Hannah's life was at stake.

Hannah hurried to her bedroom, where she stood in front of her open closet for at least five minutes, trying to decide what to wear. Then she shook her head at her indecision. She usually had no problem making a selection. Jeans and a T-shirt or button-up blouse. She lived on a ranch. That's what people wore.

Then why was she digging into the back of her closet for the sundresses she'd worn during her summer months at the university? She pulled out a pale blue dress she hadn't worn in years and shook off the dust.

The fabric was the same color as her eyes, one boy had said when she'd worn it on campus. She'd received several wolf-whistles that day. Even now, her cheeks heated at the memory.

She smoothed her hand over the material. The garment had hugged every curve of her body and swished around her legs, making her feel the most feminine she had in her entire life. Amy, her roommate, made her buy it for a night on the town with her girlfriends. She'd never danced so much in her life.

So, she loved the fabric and the way it felt against her skin, but who was she trying to impress?

Immediately, an image of Taz filled her thoughts.

Oh, hell no.

He was a client, not a potential date. Perhaps she'd wear it to dinner and then go to Eagle Rock for a night on the town. Ha! She'd really impress the toothless old ranchers who frequented the Blue Moose Tavern.

She started to put the dress back in the closet, but her hand halted halfway there. The dress was pretty, and it looked good on her.

On the other hand, the guys would comment. They might even make fun of her.

But what did she care?

Hannah pulled the dress off the hanger, fished in her underwear drawer for the sexy thong panties her friend had insisted she buy to go with the dress. She claimed they wouldn't leave a panty line. Adding the matching bra to her collection, she squared her shoulders and twisted her door handle.

Before she could change her mind, she ran across the hall and hung the dress on the hook on the back of the door. Then she stripped out of her filthy clothes and climbed into the shower.

As the water sluiced over her skin, her thoughts took a detour to the hot new client who'd shown up out of nowhere and knocked her off balance. Not only was he ruggedly handsome, he had a way with animals like no other. Well, except maybe Gavin. The way he'd calmed Bella and helped with the goat and the puppy had earned major points in Hannah's book.

He's a client. Which translates to OFF LIMITS.

Using a bit of the floral-scented shampoo, she scrubbed her head, working out all of the manure and straw from her tangled hair. She was doing it for herself, not for *him*. She didn't like smelling like a horse.

But, if a man wanted to run his hands through her hair and maybe press a kiss to her forehead, he wouldn't want to get a mouthful of horse crap.

Not that she had a particular man in mind.

Again, unbidden, Taz's image jumped to the forefront.

She could shoot Gavin for bringing up her need to date. If he hadn't, she'd still be trudging along, happy to be single and unaware of the potential a certain man might have in bed.

After rinsing the suds out of her hair, she scrubbed her body and adjusted the water cooler to rinse off. By the time she stepped out of the shower, she was chilled and ready to face the man without any lingering heat at her core.

Until she slipped into the bra and panties and stood in front of the mirror. She wasn't quite the college coed she'd been. Her body was leaner and tighter from the hard work she put into the ranch.

Why shouldn't she have someone in her life? Someone she could hold at night and make love to? The chill disappeared in a flash, her body heating from within. A man whose hands would skim across every curve and angle, leaving trails of kisses everywhere.

She moaned, running her own hands over her skin. How wonderful would she feel to have a man's coarse hands touch her all over?

Sweet Jesus. What was she thinking?

Hannah grabbed the blow dryer and went to work on her hair, which she normally let dry naturally, except during the coldest days of winter. She smoothed each strand, pulling the tresses straight. They hung past her shoulders in a golden sheath. She'd been meaning to go to the hairdresser in Eagle Rock to get it cut to a more manageable length. But now, she was glad she hadn't.

When she slipped the dress over her head and let it fall down around her hips, she sighed.

Pushing back her shoulders, she stepped out of the bathroom and was halfway down the hall to the stairs when she remembered she hadn't put on any shoes.

Her cheeks burning, she ran back to her bedroom, glad no one, namely *him,* had caught her all dressed up and barefoot. Not that guys noticed fashion faux pas. Still, she slipped into a low-heeled pair of strappy sandals, cast a quick glance in the mirror and headed downstairs at a more sedate pace.

Voices boomed from the direction of the kitchen. As she reached the bottom of the steps, she paused, losing her nerve.

Lori emerged from the living room carrying a cardboard box. "Oh, there you are," she said and then motioned with her head toward the contents of the box. "The puppy has a full belly and is sleeping for now. I thought I'd take him with me, in case he cries."

Hannah smiled. The puppy was buried in layers of an old fleece blanket with nothing but his nose sticking out. "Aren't you afraid someone will step on him?"

"I'll put him in the corner where I sit." Lori frowned. "Unless you think someone will fall on him. I'd hate for someone to squish the little guy."

Hannah shook her head. "I'm sure he'll be fine."

Lori turned back to the living room. "On second thought, I'll leave him in the living room. I eat fast, anyway."

Hannah headed for the kitchen, surprised

Lori hadn't mentioned anything about the dress.

Maybe no one else would notice the change in attire.

"Oh, Hannah?" Lori stopped before crossing into the living area. "You look really pretty in that dress. You should wear them more often."

Hannah's cheeks burned, and she stammered, "Thanks." Fortunately, Lori's focus had already returned to the pup.

Now hesitant to enter the all-male domain, Hannah debated running back upstairs to change into her usual jeans and a T-shirt

"Oh, good. You're here." Percy emerged from kitchen. "We were waiting to start dinner until you and Lori made it to the table."

"You never have to wait on me. Those men have to be hungry."

Percy frowned. "You know we always wait for the whole crew when we have a newcomer to the ranch. And you get the honor of introducing him."

Right. How could she forget? She'd made it one of the traditions of the rehab ranch. Every guest was introduced to the rest of the clients and fulltime staff at his or her first dinner.

This one time, she wished she hadn't established the tradition.

Forcing a smile to her stiff lips, she entered the kitchen with Percy, her pulse racing.

Franklin and Vasquez whistled, and Gavin chuckled.

"Wow," Young said from his seat at the

table. "Who knew our own Miss Kendricks was such a hot chick?"

"I know, right?" Franklin started forward. "Let me get your chair."

Taz stepped behind Hannah and placed a hand at the small of her back. "I've got it." He pulled out her chair and waited while she took her seat.

The rest of the clients and staff settled at the big trestle table, loaded with a tray of grilled steaks, chicken breasts and several side dishes of macaroni and cheese, baked beans and corn on the cob. A large Dutch oven contained baked potatoes.

"How did you manage to pull all of this together so fast?"

Taz nodded toward Percy and Gavin. "I had a little help."

"The food smells delicious." Hannah waved to the others standing around the table, and they all took a seat.

Taz sat beside her.

His big thigh bumped against hers, sending shockwaves through her and heat rushing to her center.

Percy touched her arm. "Hannah, are you starting this party?"

Hannah nodded and cleared her throat. "I'd like to welcome the newest addition to our guests here at the Brighter Days Rehab Ranch. Please give Alex Davila, former Army Ranger, a warm welcome."

Everyone said hello, even though most of them had already met him out at the barn. One by one, the others went around the table introducing themselves to Taz, giving him a brief description of who they were, where they were from and why they were there.

Taz listened, acknowledged and asked questions as they introduced themselves.

Hannah was impressed at how he met each individual's gaze and how his questions brought a smile. The man had them laughing and joking by the time they passed around the platter of steaks, cooked to perfection.

"Oh, and you can call me Taz," he said.

"I'll call you anything you want me to call you, as long as you always cook my steak like this. You're hired as permanent grill master," Gavin said between bites of juicy, tender steak.

"Just don't ask me to turn on a stove. I wouldn't know how," Taz said, with a shake of his head.

"Who needs sides, anyway?" Young said, shoveling another bite of steak into his mouth and moaning.

Lori finished her meal quickly. "Please excuse me. I want to check on Lucky."

"Lucky?" Franklin laughed. "You named that mutt Lucky?"

"What's lucky about your mother refusing to feed you?" Vasquez asked.

Lori rose from her chair. "He's lucky someone who cared enough to save him found him before he died."

Vasquez nodded. "He is lucky you found him."

"It's a good name for the little guy," Young said. "At least now he has a fighting chance."

Lori smiled. "I hope so. He's got me batting on his team."

After Lori left the room, Percy glanced at Gavin. "Speaking of luck, did you ever figure out why the tractor brakes gave out on Hannah the other day?"

Gavin nodded, his gaze capturing Hannah's. "Yeah."

"And?" Percy prodded.

Talk died down at the table.

Gavin's lips pursed. "Someone tampered with them."

Though she already knew about the tampered brakes, Hannah pressed a hand to her churning belly. Somehow, announcing it aloud made it more real.

Percy's brows descended. "Who could have done it?" He turned his head, staring at the guests at the table.

Franklin raised his hand. "I didn't. I wouldn't know a brake from a whatchamacallit."

Vasquez held up his hand. "I know what a brake is on a HUMMV, but this is the first time I've been around tractors. Besides, I like Miss Kendricks. Why would I want to hurt her?"

"Wasn't me," Young said.

"Nor me," Lori said from the doorway,

carrying the puppy pressed to her chest.

"If not any of us, then who?" Percy asked.

"We hired a few hands that day to help load hay," Gavin reminded him. "We need to question them."

Percy nodded. "Mark Bradley, Abe Foster and Troy Nash."

"I need to go into town tomorrow," Hannah said. "If I run into any of them, I'll ask."

"What will you ask?" Gavin shook his head and in a falsetto voice, he mimicked her, "Excuse me, did you sabotage my tractor in an attempt to kill me?"

Hannah shrugged. "I don't know. But if one of them has a problem with me, maybe I'll see the guilt in his face?"

"Miss Kendricks, you need to stay clear of them if you think they want to hurt you," Lori said. "This ranch wouldn't be what it is without you."

"She's right," Young said. "We all need you."

"Speak for yourself," Franklin said.

Vasquez elbowed him in the side. "Shut the fuck up. You know you like Miss Kendricks. She's all that, besides, she puts up with your whiny ass."

Franklin's face turned a ruddy red. "Okay, so maybe we all care about you, Miss Kendricks. Not one of us wants to see you hurt."

"We can go to town and ask around," Young offered.

Hannah couldn't believe her clients would do this for her. She shook her head. "Absolutely not.

You're guests here. I won't have you putting yourselves in danger because of a few accidents involving me."

"Ma'am," Vasquez said, "they don't sound like accidents. Someone's got it in for you."

Hannah sighed. That's what she was afraid of, too.

"And we don't want anything to happen to you," Franklin said. "We've got your back, Miss Kendricks."

Hannah's gaze swept around the table. Every guest, her staff, and Lori nodded, demonstrating their desire to protect her. She swallowed the lump in her throat.

She didn't have to turn to the new guy to know where he stood. While the others had been talking, Taz's hand had slipped beneath the table to capture hers.

Her heart swelled. If someone had it in for her, he'd have to go through an army of former military. She prayed the situation wouldn't come to that.

Chapter 8

Taz liked the feel of Hannah's hand in his, and he didn't want to let go. But when the others rose from the table he had to, or they'd notice and comment. And Hannah wouldn't want anyone to know he'd been holding her hand. Displays of affection between her and a client went against her personal code of conduct.

At that moment, Taz felt the pressing need to make a phone call. Hank had to know about the hired hands. He could be running background checks on them while Taz kept watch over Hannah.

When Franklin and Vasquez offered to pull cleanup duty in the kitchen, Taz excused himself and went to his room to make that phone call. He pulled out his cell phone and checked the reception. Nothing. No service.

But he needed to get a call through to Hank. In order to make that call, he either had to drive into Eagle Rock or use the ranch's landline. He'd noted a cordless phone on a table in the entrance near the stairs. He remembered seeing others scattered throughout the house. He'd have to take the risk of someone lifting one of the other phones and hearing him talking to Hank.

Taz paced his room for several minutes thinking through his options and cursing the limitations of modern technology. He'd have to wait until those who lived in the house went to bed. Only then could he be sure no one else would listen in.

He might as well get a shower while he waited, making it quick so that he could get back downstairs to keep an eye on Hannah.

Grabbing clean jeans, he ducked across the hallway into the shared bathroom and took a cold shower. It accomplished two things: first, it cooled any heat lingering low in his belly from holding Hannah's hand. Second, it saved time waiting for the water to warm.

He was back downstairs in ten minutes, clean, if a little damp. He found Hannah in the living room, seated in a rocking chair, holding the rejected puppy against her breast. "What happened to Lori?" he asked.

"She went to the barn to check on the other puppies to make sure Sydney didn't reject any of those remaining." Hannah spoke in hushed, gentle tones. "I told her I'd watch out for Lucky while she was out there."

"Did she go by herself?" Taz asked.

"No. I made her take Gavin." Her lips pressed into a tight line. "I would hate if someone mistook her for me and...well...I didn't want her to be hurt."

Taz settled in on the sofa nearby, grateful for the opportunity to talk. "What do you know about the men you hired to help haul hay?"

She smiled. "Abe and Mark are recent high

school graduates earning money during the summer. They start college this fall." Her lips turned downward. "Troy Nash is the neighbor's son. I've known him all my life."

Taz leaned forward resting his elbows on his knees. "Does any one of them have a reason to want to harm you?"

Hannah shook her head.

"Think hard," Taz insisted. "Have you done anything that might have angered them or someone they care about?"

Her brows dipped. "I was away at college for four years, but I've been back for the past three. And, up until the past couple of weeks, nothing strange has happened. Then, all of a sudden, things started going wrong."

Taz tensed. "Besides the tractor brakes, tell me about the other two events?"

Hannah shrugged and explained about the rail in the loft and the cut girth strap on her personal saddle. "They could have been accidents," she said, her voice trailing off. "Okay, so maybe they weren't."

Taz's lips twitched. Patterson had said she'd scoff at the attempts. "Even if the first two incidents were accidents, according to Blackstock, the tractor brakes didn't give out on their own."

Hannah stroked the tiny animal lying so quietly against her. "Why would someone want to hurt me? I can't remember making anyone mad enough to want to kill me. Not Abe, Mark or Troy. And I work with the clients on the ranch every day. Nothing they've said or done would indicate a deep-seated hatred." She stared across at him. "But none of that should worry you. You're here to recuperate. I won't let my troubles affect you."

"If I don't have something else to think about, I'll sit around racking my brain for the memories that refuse to surface." He touched her knee. "Worrying about you will take my mind off my own problems. My therapist back at Walter Reed said that if I can quit forcing my memories to come back, maybe they'd return when I least expect them."

Hannah shook her head well before he finished his argument. "I can't let you get in the middle of this. I would never forgive myself if something happened to one of my clients because someone was aiming for me."

"Let *me* worry about me."

"But that's *my* job," Hannah said, her brows furrowing.

"Not anymore. I'm making it my job to look out for you."

"No." She shook her head. "Absolutely not." The rocker moved faster.

"It's either me, Franklin, Vasquez or Young." He took her free hand. "You need someone to watch your back. Who would you rather have?"

"I could get Gavin to cover me. Or Percy."

"They both have work to do. I'm new here. So far, you don't have me assigned to any other task. I could work alongside you and make sure you don't miss anything in front of or behind where you're working."

"You're not supposed to be helping me. I'm supposed to be helping you."

"By letting me help you, you will be helping me." He leaned toward her. "I need this." And he did. He needed to be needed and in such a way as to use the skills he'd honed on the battlefield. He'd been good at assessing dangerous situations and determining the best courses of action. He squeezed her hand. "Let me help you, pretty Hannah."

She sighed. "I have to admit, after the tractor incident, I've been a little hesitant to go out on the ranch on my own."

"And you shouldn't."

"But I can't expect you to dog my every footstep."

His lips curled upward on the corner. "Trust me, following you won't be a hardship. Especially when you wear a dress like that."

Her cheeks turned pink. "I was wondering if you noticed."

"The moment you stepped into the kitchen." His gaze skimmed over the blue fabric and rose to her face. "That dress is the same color as your eyes."

The red in her cheeks darkened. "Thank you. This outfit makes me feel less like one of the ranch hands and more like a woman."

"Oh, sweetheart, you couldn't look like one of the guys if you tried."

The back door slammed shut and a voice called out, "I'm back."

Hannah pulled her hand free of Taz's.

Lori rushed into the living room, breathless. "I checked on the puppies. She still had eight. All of them were nursing and seemed to be doing fine." She stopped short when she noticed Taz sitting on the couch. "Sorry. Did I interrupt something?"

"Not at all." Hannah pushed to her feet and handed the puppy to Lori. "He could use another round of milk. Do you need a hand?"

Lori shook her head. "No. I can handle it by myself. Lucky knows what the syringe means now and doesn't resist. I don't want to keep you up."

"I don't mind," Hannah said. "Come get me if you need someone to take over for a couple hours."

Taz stood beside Hannah, knowing that if she got up in the night to help with the puppy, he'd be up, as well. He'd have to keep his bedroom door open in order to hear her movements. Keeping track of Hannah would be easier if they were sharing a bedroom. He almost laughed out loud. He could just imagine her reaction if he asked to spend the night in her room.

Then he realized how much he would like that. He doubted they would get much sleep.

As Hannah started toward the stairs, Gavin emerged from the office.

"I just got off the phone with the veterinarian. He said he's headed to town for an emergency call. He can meet you at the Blue Moose on his way through if you can get there in fifteen minutes. I'd go, but I promised to help Young with a special project before lights out."

"I'm on my way." Hannah snatched a jacket from the hall closet and her keys and wallet and hurried toward the door.

Gavin stepped in front of her and held up a hand. "You can't go alone."

"I'm going with her," Taz said.

"In that case." Gavin nodded and moved aside. "Be careful and watch for deer and moose on the road."

Hannah headed out the door and down the front porch steps and turned toward the old farm truck.

Taz hooked her arm. "I'll drive."

"But—"

"I promise, you can tell me how to drive, when to turn and even yell if I'm going too fast. But I'm driving." He led her to the truck Hank assigned him and held the door so she could climb up into the passenger seat.

They accomplished the trip to town in comfortable silence. The route was easy to follow, and they arrived at the Blue Moose Tavern with two minutes to spare.

Taz shifted into park and glanced around, searching for anyone who appeared suspicious or dangerous. Nobody jumped out of the darkness or stirred in the shadows. Fairly confident Hannah would be safe, he turned to her. "Should we wait outside or go in?"

"He might have beat us here. Let's go in and see." Hannah opened her door and was on the ground before Taz could get around the truck.

"You know, you're killing old-fashioned chivalry. At least let me escort you inside." He held out his elbow.

She smiled and shook her head. "I'm so used to doing everything for myself."

"And I admire that in you. But, humor me. You're a beautiful lady in a pretty dress. A man should open doors for you."

She raised her brows. "But not in my jeans and T-shirt?"

"Sweetheart, you could be covered in horse manure and mud and I'd still open the door for you."

Her laugh echoed in the darkness.

The joyful sound made his heart lighter. He pushed open the door to the tavern and waited for her to enter—almost like they were on a date. If they didn't have to get back to the ranch with the formula for the puppy, he'd buy her a drink, and they could talk and get to know each other better.

Then he reminded himself that he wasn't there to date her. He was there to protect her.

Once inside the tavern, Taz slipped an arm around her waist and pulled her close, his gaze sweeping the room for potential threats.

"Aren't you pushing the chivalry a little overboard?" she asked.

"Is my arm bothering you?"

She hesitated and then answered softly, "No."

"Do you see the veterinarian?"

She pushed up onto her tiptoes and looked around the room. "No."

"Do you want to wait outside or sit at the bar?"

"Let's sit at the bar." She smiled up at him. "Doing that would make Gavin happy."

Taz frowned. "Why would sitting at the bar make Gavin happy? He's not even here."

"It would be almost like a date." She shrugged. "I promised him I'd get out and date. But this isn't really a date." She blushed and she stepped away. "Never mind."

"Hey, if it makes you feel any better, I had the same thought coming through the door. I was thinking, if we weren't in a hurry, I could buy you a drink."

She stopped and looked back at the bar. "Well, it's been a long time since I came here for a drink. And I do like a good beer, or even a glass of wine. But I can pay for my own."

"Shh. You're killing my ego again." He led her to the bar and waited while she took a seat. "And I'm buying a pretty lady a drink." He waited for her to open her mouth and argue. When she didn't, he smiled. "What? You're not going all tough-gal on me?"

Hannah shook her head. "I'd like a glass of red wine."

"Any particular kind of red wine?"

"Whatever the bartender recommends. Just make it dry."

Taz ordered her wine and a glass of ginger ale for himself.

Hannah lifted her glass of wine. "You're not having a beer?"

He shook his head. "I'm the designated driver." Alcohol and surveillance didn't mix. He was on the job, meaning, he needed a clear head.

"Good call." She lifted her glass to his. "Here's to getting back old memories and making new ones."

Taz stared into her clear blue eyes. How he wished he could get back at least the memory of what happened just before the explosion. Suddenly he wished he could make some new memories with someone as strong and vibrant as the woman on the other side of the wine glass.

She took a sip and set her glass on the counter. "There he is." Hannah slipped off her barstool and hurried toward the door where a man, dressed in jeans and a faded chambray shirt, stood looking around the room.

When he spotted her, he grinned and held his arms wide.

Hannah fell into them, and they hugged like old friends.

Taz followed a few steps behind Hannah, his fists clenching. Something about the man hugging

126

the pretty therapist made the anger rise up, strong and hard. He wanted to step between them and maybe even pound on the man smiling at her.

But he knew he couldn't, and he used the breathing techniques the counselor at Bethesda had recommended. Breathe deeply in through the nose and let it out through the mouth.

Hannah stepped back and waved Taz closer. "Taz, this is Dr. David Waters, our local veterinarian." She smiled at the doctor and said, "Dave, this is Alex Davila, my—"

"—date tonight." Taz held out his hand. "But you can call me Taz."

Hannah's brow wrinkled, but she didn't correct him. Instead, she turned to the vet. "So, Dave, how're Natalie and the baby?"

The doctor grinned. "Wonderful. Liam is growing so fast. He's already sitting up by himself, and he's always smiling and laughing. Natalie and I love being parents." He touched his hand to the pocket on his shirt. "Oh, I have something for you." He pulled a small bottle from his pocket that looked more like a child's toy for a doll. "The puppy should be able to use this. And if you follow me out to my truck, I have a package of formula that should last a week."

"Do you have time to join us for a drink?" Hannah asked.

Before she finished asking, the doctor was shaking his head. "Can't. Mr. Rausch has a cow down with a calf stuck in the birth canal. I need to get out there before he loses both." He turned toward the door.

Hannah followed.

Taz brought up the rear.

Dr. Waters handed over the formula and gave Hannah one last hug. He held out his hand to Taz. "I'm glad to see Hannah dating. Take care of her, will ya?"

Taz nodded. "I will."

In a hurry to get to his urgent call, the veterinarian climbed into his truck and drove away.

Hannah turned back to Taz. "Why did you tell him you were my date?"

He grinned, held the door open for her to enter the tavern and said, "That way you have proof for Gavin that we were on a date. He'll never know the difference unless we tell."

And Hannah would never know the truth about why Taz told Dr. Waters she was his date. In his own way, he'd staked his claim. If he wasn't mistaken, that little blast of rage had been something too akin to jealousy for his liking. And he really had no claim on Hannah.

Placing his hand in the small of her back, he guided her to the truck.

A movement caught his attention out of the corner of his eye.

At the same time, Hannah stiffened and leaned to the right, peering around the hood of the truck. "Did you see that?"

His pulse leapt and he pushed Hannah behind him. Reaching for the nine-millimeter pistol beneath his jacket, he took cover behind the truck hood.

A shadowy figure glanced their way and then ducked between two buildings.

The way the man moved struck a cord of familiarity with Taz. He also swore he might have recognized his face. But like his recurring nightmare, he couldn't put a name to it. It niggled at the back of his mind, tugging at those untapped memories he couldn't quite access. He knew they meant something. Something important.

Hannah sighed. "For a moment, I thought I saw someone lurking by the corner of the general store. It's probably all of this conspiracy stuff, making me jumpy."

"I saw him, too." Taz's pulse thumped hard against his veins and his forehead broke out in a sweat. He could smell the dust of Afghanistan and feel the weight of the wall lying against his chest. "Did you see who it was?"

"Not clearly. It could have been someone I know, or a stranger. Eagle Rock might be small, but we get occasional visitors."

His moves jerky, his attention still on the corner, Taz held open the passenger door and waited while Hannah climbed in.

As far as Taz was concerned, Troy Nash had been at the top of the list of suspects. He had been there early that morning Hannah's brakes had been sabotaged. He probably knew his way around a tractor, having grown up on a ranch. He knew the type of terrain the tractor would be working on, and the damage that sabotaged brakes would mean to the driver.

Taz needed to get word to Hank. Being with Hannah made it hard for him to get to a phone alone. He considered returning to the tavern to borrow a phone, but leaving Hannah in the truck by herself was out of the question.

He'd have to try at the ranch house. In the meantime, he checked over the truck. If the shadowy figure wanted to hurt Hannah, he might have damaged the vehicle in which she'd arrived.

As far as Taz could tell in the dark, holding only a small flashlight, the truck appeared untouched or tampered with.

He climbed in, held his breath and started the engine. He counted to five and let go of the breath. What had he expected? They hadn't been inside the tavern long enough for someone to plant a bomb. Just because a guy knew how to damage brakes didn't mean he knew how to wire an explosive.

"You thought he might have sabotaged the truck, didn't you?" Hannah asked, her voice quiet, her face pale in the light from the dash.

"Doesn't hurt to be cautious."

She shook her head. "I don't like this. I'm not the kind of person who sees the enemy in every face. I can't even tell when someone is lying to me. I *trust* people."

Taz took that hit to his gut. He deserved it, after lying to her from the start about his reason for being at Brighter Days. What was done, was done. At this point, he couldn't take back the lie, nor would it help Hannah.

He shifted into gear and pulled out of the parking lot. He shot a glance toward Hannah. "Until we find out who's at the bottom of the threats, I suggest you be a little less trusting."

For the remainder of the ride back to the ranch, she sat in silence.

When they arrived, he touched her arm. "Stay put for just a moment."

Using the high-beam flashlight he'd found in the console, Taz checked the near vicinity, shining the beam into the bushes and at the outbuildings. When he was relatively sure the area was safe, he opened her door and helped her down.

Taz offered her his arm. He didn't like seeing this woman who was usually upbeat and take-charge so depressed by what had happened. He was there to protect her, but he also wanted to take away the pain of betrayal she surely must be feeling.

He liked this woman more than any woman he'd ever come into contact with. Perhaps too much to be effective guarding her from trouble.

Hannah was saddened by the thought someone she knew might be attacking her. Thankfully, she had Taz with her, and he'd be there for the near term. Though she didn't like relying on anyone, she felt safe with the newest client on the ranch. His broad shoulders and solid physique could intimidate lesser men. His muscles and brawn intimidated her.

Well, not so much intimidated. Her reaction to him scared her as much as it excited her.

Inside the house, the lights had all been turned off except one in the foyer near the staircase.

Hannah led the way up the stairs, so aware of Taz walking behind her that she tripped on the last step.

Taz caught her around the waist and steadied her.

"I'm usually not this clumsy," she muttered. Great, she just admitted that he flustered her. "I mean, I'm pretty sure-footed. I must be tired." Not in lust over the new man on the ranch.

"No worries. I told you, I have your back."

"In this case, I can't argue." Then again, she wouldn't have been so hyper-aware of the man behind her if he weren't there. Then she might not have tripped.

"What's the plan for tomorrow?" he asked.

"We have a field of hay Percy cut two days ago that needs to be baled and moved. It's supposed to start raining in the afternoon, so we'll need to be up and going early in the morning."

"I'll be ready." Taz stopped in front of his room.

Hannah's was one door farther along the landing. She hesitated, not really wanting to leave him yet, but she didn't have a reason to keep him up any longer. Resigned to saying goodnight, she started to turn.

Taz captured her hand before she could walk away. "Promise you won't go anywhere without me."

She frowned, not at all comfortable with him being her personal bodyguard. The independent woman inside resisted being coddled or treated differently than anyone else. Especially by one of the guests. "Should someone take another shot at me, I don't like the idea of you being in the line of fire."

"Hey." He pressed a finger to her lips. "Let's not rehash this discussion. Think of it as my therapy. I need to be needed, and your situation is just the kind of problem I'm suited to handle."

"But—" she said against his finger.

He dipped his head close to his finger. "Shh. You can argue all you want. I'm sticking to you like a second skin." Then he dropped his finger from her lips and kissed her like a conquering hero, claiming her mouth as his prize.

As quickly as the kiss began, it ended. He straightened, spun her around and gave her a gentle nudge in the small of her back. "Go to bed, Hannah. Tomorrow will be a busy day."

Her lips still tingling, Hannah ran for her door, afraid if she stuck around, she'd turn back and kiss him again.

Once she was inside her bedroom with the door closed, she leaned her back on it and slid to the floor. She pressed her fingers to her lips and drew in a deep breath. This was not happening. It couldn't. He was a client.

Now was not a good time for her hormones to rebel and take over. She prided herself on following the rules, even if they were rules she'd made for herself.

After a few minutes, she got to her feet, shed her clothes and slipped into one of her nicer nightgowns. Normally, she slept in an oversized T-shirt and jogging shorts. If she were smart, she'd continue with her normal routine to remind her who she was.

The thought of Taz only inches away on the other side of her bedroom wall made her choose the sexy black nightgown with the matching panties. They'd been a birthday gift from Amy, the same friend who'd chosen the blue dress for her. This would be the first time she'd actually worn the gift. She'd always thought she wasn't the right girl to wear it, never feeling sexy enough to pull off the outfit.

Tonight, after that kiss, Hannah's understanding of herself had made a complete turnaround. She'd gone from one of the guys to a sex-kitten wannabe. She'd never known she had that kind of sensuality in her, always thinking maybe she lacked the ultra-feminine gene a woman needed to be sexy.

One man and his kisses had shown her a side of herself she didn't know existed, which scared the crap out of her. And it left her so excited, she ached low in her belly.

She pulled back her comforter and lay on top of the sheets, too hot in the skimpy baby-doll nightgown to cover up.

Footsteps sounded in the hallway outside her doorway.

Hannah bolted upright in the bed, her pulse hammering through her veins, her breath seized in her lungs.

Did the footsteps belong to *him*?

Should she cover up?

Had she locked the door?

Thoughts raced through her head.

A knock sounded.

Hannah clamped a hand over her mouth to keep from yelping. When she had herself under control, she answered in her smoothest, and hopefully, sexiest tone. "Yes?"

The door opened.

Hannah's heart lodged in her throat.

Gavin poked his head through the crack. "Are you up for hauling hay—" he caught one look at her and grinned. "Holy shit! Who's that for?" He stepped through the door, leaving it open and swept the room with his gaze. "Or is there someone under your bed?"

Hannah yanked the sheet up, covering her body. "No one is under my bed. I just...didn't have any clean T-shirts." Her cheeks burned with the lie.

Gavin's eyes widened. "No, wait. You were waiting for someone else, weren't you? Perhaps someone in the next room?" He gave a low wolf-whistle.

"No, I wasn't. You've got it all wrong."

Would the embarrassment never cease?

"Right." Gavin nodded, his grin widening. "I sure hope he appreciates what he's getting."

Heat spread from Hannah's chest up into her face and all the way out to her ears. She yanked the comforter over herself and up to her chin. "You did this," she yelled in a whisper.

"Uh-uh, darlin', you did this all by yourself. Never knew you had it in you to clean up so pretty."

"No. You put *him* in the room next to me on purpose, didn't you?"

"Oh, that." Gavin grinned. "Guilty. And it's turning out just like I planned, based on the sexy nightie."

"Everything okay in here?" Taz's voice preceded him into Hannah's room. He stepped in behind Gavin. "Hannah, are you all right?"

"Sweet Jesus!" She pulled the comforter over her head.

"She's just feeling a little out of character," Gavin said.

"I can hear you," Hannah said.

"You should ask her to go for a walk in the moonlight," Gavin suggested. "The stars are pretty impressive tonight.

Hannah pushed the comforter from her face and flung a pillow at the Gavin.

Gavin ducked and the pillow hit Taz in the face.

"Get out," Hannah said through gritted teeth.

Gavin laughed out loud. "I'm going. I'm going. I know when three's a crowd." He stepped past Taz. "You, on the other hand, don't have to leave so quickly. I believe Miss Sexy-in-her-black-nighty would like you to stay."

Gavin was halfway through the door when Hannah hit him with a pillow, this time her aim being true.

"You can thank me later," he called out from the landing.

Taz's gaze swung from the open doorway to Hannah. "What was that all about?"

Mortified, Hannah pulled the comforter up to her chin. "Nothing. Gavin's just a juvenile in a grownup body."

"No, I'm just looking out for my friend," he called out, his footsteps moving away. "At least one of us should be getting some." A door shut at the other end of the hallway.

Taz's brows twisted. "Do I want to know what that was all about?"

Hannah shook her head, her cheeks still burning hot. If the man would ever leave, she'd change into a T-shirt and shorts and burn the black nightgown. Sexy, she was not.

"Are you sure you're okay?"

"I'm fine. Perfectly fine," she said through clenched teeth and forced a smile sure to appear more like a grimace.

"Goodnight, Hannah." He turned away.

Hannah released the breath she'd been holding and relaxed her death grip on the comforter. Finally, he was leaving her to die of embarrassment in solitude.

As he stepped across the threshold, he turned back and winked. "By the way, that black thing you're wearing..." He shook his head.

Hannah's heart dipped into her belly.

A smile spread across Taz's face. "Wow." And he was gone.

Chapter 9

Taz rose before daylight to get a head start on Hannah. That, and he couldn't sleep anyway. Not with her in the next room wearing a sinfully delicious nightgown he'd only caught a teasing glimpse of.

Through the night, all he could think about was taking it off her, one strap at a time and licking her skin from the curve of her graceful neck to the swells of her full breasts and lower still.

Knowing she was inches away on the other side of the wall kept him hard and ready for more than he should even consider. She was the job. Hank was counting on him to protect her. Not jump in her bed and make sweet love to that gorgeous body.

Taz headed first for the bathroom, splashed his face with cold water and brushed his teeth. He wanted to get out to the barn and go over the tractor, baling machine, truck and trailer they'd use that day to make sure no one had tampered with them.

When he left the bathroom, he paused in front of Hannah's bedroom and cocked his head to the side, listening. Based on the muted sounds, she was awake and moving around.

He was tempted to knock on the door and

see if she answered, wearing that black nightgown. And if she would invite him in.

A sound down the hallway made him straighten and hurry away from her door. He didn't need to be caught ogling the therapist. Though, based on Blackstock's behavior the night before, Hannah's friend was trying to hook them up.

Why Blackstock thought Hannah needed a friend to set her up, Taz didn't know. The woman was beautiful inside and out. She didn't need help getting a date. In fact, she probably had men waiting in line to be with her.

As Taz headed out of the house, he passed the living room.

Lori was just adjusting the strap on her prosthetic leg. When she had it in place, she rose from the lounge chair. "Oh, hi." Her cheeks reddened.

Taz hadn't meant to embarrass the woman. He would have walked on by, but now that she'd acknowledge him, he wanted to find out about Lucky. "How's the puppy?"

She smiled. "He made it through the night, with the dog replacement formula you and Hannah brought home last night. Still, I'm worried it's not enough. I spoke with Gavin. I'm going to take the little guy to the vet today and get whatever else he needs. I'll also try to put him with his mother, again. Her milk would be best for him."

"It's good to know he has you to look out

for him."

"We all need someone who cares," she said as she lifted the puppy out of the box beside the chair. "Don't we?"

Taz's chest tightened. He was reminded of the children's Christmas movie about Rudolf when they visited the island of misfit toys. Wasn't that what Brighter Days Rehab Ranch was? An island of misfits in a sea of normal people?

Taz almost felt guilty for taking up space at the facility when all his limbs were intact. Lori, Franklin, Vasquez and Young had life so much worse.

The only thing missing on Taz was a few minutes of memory. "You have a big heart, Lori. The puppy really is Lucky."

She smiled. "Thank you."

As he turned to leave, Lori called out, "Taz?"

"Yes, ma'am?"

"You'll look out for Hannah today, won't you?"

He nodded. "You bet."

"She's an amazing woman. If you want to talk about big hearts, she beats us all." Her cheeks flushed. "Just so you know. We all care about her."

"From what I can tell, she cares about all of you. I'll stay close."

"Thanks."

He left Lori in the living room and passed through the kitchen where Cookie had bacon frying in a skillet.

The older cook, with tattoos running from his wrists up his arms to disappear under his T-shirt, nodded a greeting. "Coffee's ready when you are."

"Thanks." Taz had planned on skipping breakfast and coffee, but the aroma lured him to the carafe of steaming brew. He poured a cup and took a sip.

"I hear you grilled a mean steak last night," Cookie said as he cracked eggs into a mixing bowl and stirred with a whisk. "I like a good steak. I'd have stayed for dinner, but my sister in Bozeman expects me on my night off. She lives alone."

The cook poured the mixture of eggs into a large skillet and set it on the gas stove. Then he turned, wiped his hands on a towel and held out one. "Carl Fite. Most folks call me Cookie."

Taz shook the cook's hand. "Alex Davila. My friends call me Taz."

Cookie snorted. "Tasmanian Davila?" Then he nodded. "I get it. So Taz, you have both arms and you're not limping. What brings you to Brighter Days?"

Trust the cook to shoot a straight question at him. "TBI. Memory loss. I'm hoping the peace and quiet of the ranch and countryside will help me to recover some missing pieces of my memory."

"Traumatic brain injuries can be tricky. Had a friend of mine suffered from that after playing football through high school." Cookie grabbed a spatula and stirred the eggs in the pan. "Changed his personality. In his case, not for the better. He ended up having a terrible temper. Two marriages and two divorces later, he lives alone."

Taz winced. "Yeah, I've been struggling with the anger issues. Again, I hope the environment here will give me a chance to recognize the triggers and control them."

"You and me both." Cookie gave him a narrow-eyed glance. "Miss Kendricks is a good person. I'd hate to see her hurt by anyone with anger management problems."

Surrounded by people who cared about her, Hannah shouldn't have been targeted for aggression.

"I'll do my best to control my temper," Taz promised. He took another sip of the coffee and set the mug in the sink. "Good coffee. If anyone asks, I'll be out at the barn."

Taz left the house and hurried across the yard to the barn as the sun rose high enough to light the sky a pre-dawn gray. The sun wouldn't top the peaks surrounding the ranch and shine down into the valley for another half hour.

A tractor stood in the barnyard with a baling machine attached to the back.

Percy leaned over the engine, wielding a wrench. He tightened a bolt and stood back. He spotted Taz and nodded. "You're up early."

"I wanted to check out the brakes on the tractor and truck we would be using today."

"Just finished doing that. But two sets of eyes are always better than one." Percy slapped a wrench in Taz's hand and waved toward the tractor. "You can start here. The truck is parked on the other side of the fence with the trailer already attached. Do you know much about farm equipment?"

Taz leaned over the engine. "I grew up a ranch. My father was responsible for running the equipment. He taught me a few things about engines and the mechanics of how things work. He let me rebuild an old tractor. I sold it and used the money to help buy my first truck."

"You might prove handy to have around. Here, you might need this." Percy handed Taz a flashlight.

Taz went over the tractor, inspecting gears, hydraulic hoses and the brakes. When everything checked out, he gave the baler a once-over before moving on to the truck and trailer they'd be using in the field. Everything checked out.

By the time he'd completed a thorough inspection, a truck with a toolbox on the back pulled up and two men got out.

Percy emerged from the barn.

Taz joined him to meet the newcomers.

"Ray, good to see you." Percy met the driver with a handshake. "Thanks for coming on short notice. My gray threw a shoe yesterday."

"We'll get it taken care of," Ray said and gave Percy's hand a brief shake.

The foreman nodded toward the other man. "Who've you got with you?"

Ray tipped his head toward the tall, muscular

stranger. "Bear Parker. Just out of the military. He's thinking about apprenticing with me to learn the trade."

Percy held out his hand. "Thank you for your service. We can use more farriers in these parts. At least in this line of work, you won't have people shooting at you."

Bear nodded, his face serious. "Nice to meet you." The man stood tall, his physique that of a man who put in the extra hours to maintain muscle-mass, strength and speed.

Percy turned to Taz. "We got us another new guest. Ray William, meet Taz Davila. Also fresh from the military, here for some R&R."

Taz shook hands with Ray and then Bear.

Bear gripped his hand longer than necessary, captured and held his gaze.

Taz wasn't sure what the extended handshake was all about, but he'd stick around to find out.

While the two men unloaded the tools necessary to shoe a horse, Taz held up the wrench and flashlight Percy had loaned him. "All the equipment seems in good working order. Where do you want me to put these?"

"You can set them on the desk in the tack room. I'm heading back to the house for another cup of coffee and breakfast. You coming up?"

Taz shook his head. "I'll hang around the barn and make sure no one tampers with the machinery."

"You don't have to worry about Ray. He's

good people."

"I'll keep that in mind." He leaned against the barn where he could keep an eye on the newcomers.

Percy headed to the house

Ray rounded the barn to the pasture and whistled for the horses.

Bear stood beside the truck, setting out tools. When Ray disappeared, his apprentice shot a glance at Taz and said in a low voice, "Hank sent me."

Taz's senses came to full alert. Without appearing obvious, he searched his peripheral vision for anyone close enough to hear them talking. When he'd determined it was clear, he stepped closer and lifted one of the tools, pretending to examine it. "I wanted to call last night, but I got no reception on my cell phone and using the landline runs risks of being discovered."

"That's why I'm here. Hank figured you'd have trouble communicating." He nodded and pointed to the tool Taz held. "What do you have?"

"I wanted to see if Hank had the ability to check the backgrounds of three hired hands."

"Troy, Abe and Mark?" Bear asked.

"You know about them?"

"One of our guys got it from Gavin that they were hired on for hay-hauling. Hank already ran background checks on them. Abe and Mark are clean. Troy's been in and out of trouble. Was arrested for DUI twice and had a restraining order for stalking a cheerleader in high school. He was recently fired from his job at the feed store for harassing the female customers."

Taz stiffened and his gaze narrowed. "Think he's capable of tampering with the brakes on Miss Kendricks's tractor, or loosening the rail in the loft?"

"Perfectly capable. The question is why?" Bear nodded toward the corner of the barn. "Ray's coming."

Taz resisted turning around to verify.

"Hank wanted me to pass on that they figured out who bought the ranch."

"I thought it was an investment group."

"It is, owned by US Senator James Buchanan. Hank put out some feelers in the law enforcement community and found that Buchanan was specific about hiring Miss Kendricks on as a therapist."

"Why her?"

"We don't know. We're running checks on Kendricks to see if she's had any connection with Buchanan in the past. Hank also found out Martin Holloway, the financial manager of the place, is Buchanan's stepson. Son of his current wife, Charise Holloway Buchanan."

"Think she might have caught wind of her husband asking specifically for Hannah?"

Bear took the tool from Taz. "I'm not sure what it's used for, but Ray will show me." Bear turned toward the farrier as the older man led a gray gelding to the back of the truck.

"That's right. By the end of the day, you'll know whether or not this work is right for you." Ray turned to Taz. "Are you interested in becoming a farrier, too? We really are short good ones around here."

"A good farrier is worth his weight in gold," Taz agreed. His father had said those same words a dozen years ago. "But, no. I haven't decided what I want to do in the civilian world. I'm still looking."

"Good luck on the job hunt," Ray said. "Not much call for men highly trained in the art of warfare. Unless you go to work for the sheriff's department."

Taz had a lot to chew on with the information Hank sent through Bear. He'd bet Troy Nash had something to do with the recent events involving Hannah. Question was, *why?*

He didn't have time to work the newfound knowledge or change his mind and circle back for breakfast with the rest of the ranch residents. When he glanced back at the house, he saw the staff and guests making their way to the barn.

Bringing up the rear was Hannah, dressed in jeans, a denim shirt and her cowboy hat. She moved with cool confidence, the natural sway of her hips sensuous without being overstated. She probably didn't have any idea how incredibly hot she was. In jeans or in the black nightgown, the woman was 100% female.

She clapped her hands together and smiled at the gathering. "Are we ready to haul some hay?"

Like good trainees, the guests and Gavin all shouted, "Yes, ma'am!"

Hannah shook her head with a half-smile. "Okay, then. But don't call me ma'am."

Franklin, Vasquez and Young climbed into the back of the truck. Percy drove the tractor and Gavin drove the truck. Hannah slipped across the bench seat to the middle. Taz slid in next to her, and they were off.

Cookie stood at the gate, still wearing the apron he'd had on while cooking breakfast. He saluted them as they drove through. "I'll have supper ready when you get back."

"Better make it lunch. We're knocking this out in record time. We have a storm rolling in," Gavin called out the window.

Taz glanced at the clear blue Montana sky. Not a cloud in sight. "Storm?"

Hannah nodded. "Storm's on the other side of the mountains. It'll be here this afternoon. All the more reason to get this done quickly. The weatherman called for record downfall. What we don't get out of the field will be ruined. "

The drive out to the hayfield took fifteen bumpy minutes across rutted roads. Taz held on to the oh-shit handle over the door to steady himself. He could imagine the discomfort felt by the men in the back of the truck, but they didn't show it. Each time they were thrown to one side of the bed or the other, they made jokes and laughed, each man using whatever strength he had to help the other stay upright.

"Aren't you worried about those three in the back?" Taz asked.

Hannah glanced over her shoulder. "Gavin's moving slowly enough, they'll be all right. Besides, they're working together, to keep from falling out of the truck. They're learning they can still do what they thought they couldn't."

Hannah was right. The three in the bed of the truck were doing just fine, and having fun.

Percy, driving ahead of them, made it out to the field first and immediately went to work baling the raked hay.

Gavin stopped the truck and flung open the door. "You're driving."

"The hell I am." Hannah scooted toward the driver's door. "Taz can drive. I'll load bales."

"Not happening," Taz said, sliding out of the passenger seat. "How can I cover your back, if I'm driving? Out in the open, you're a walking bull's-eye."

She chewed on her bottom lip, her gaze sweeping across the hayfield. "We need everyone to get that hay loaded and so far, bullets and shooters haven't been part of the attacks. I'm pretty sure I can take care of myself."

"Agreed, as evidence you're still alive. But humor me, will ya? Think of it as part of my—"

Hannah held up her hand. "Don't say it. Don't tell me it's all part of your therapy."

"Okay, but will you drive?"

She sighed. "Yes. But I'd rather be out there slinging bales with the rest of you."

"Noted." Taz grinned. "A driver with a hand steady on the wheel is just as important to loading hay."

"Yeah, yeah." Hannah settled behind the wheel and waited for the crew to get in position.

The morning passed without incident—for the most part. Young nearly fell from the top of the stack when he tried to haul up a bale to the highest point by himself.

Taz had to give him props for stretching to learn his limits. The man had more balls than most men with two legs.

Franklin and Vasquez tried competing against each other, but finally found that working together was much faster.

Taz discovered tossing eighty-pound bales to be good exercise. Since he didn't have to keep as close an eye on Hannah he had time to think about what Bear told him.

A senator had purchased a ranch and very specifically hired Hannah to set up the program for the veterans. He still couldn't figure out why. Or why the senator didn't want the staff to know the project was his. He hid his ownership behind an investment group. That made no sense at all. What politician would set up an organization to help wounded veterans and not claim the effort? A move like that would buy him a hell of a lot more votes.

Unless said politician had something to hide about the ranch and the connection to Miss Kendricks.

An affair?

Taz shook his head. No. Hannah wouldn't go out with a married man. Would she?

Hannah had told him she never knew her father. Could her mother have had a secret affair with the senator—twenty-eight years ago? That made more sense. He wouldn't want anyone, especially his wife to know he had a lovechild.

And why would Troy Nash want to harm Hannah? If you asked the staff and guests at the ranch, the woman was practically a saint.

Unless someone was paying Troy, who'd recently lost his job, to stir up trouble.

Taz needed to talk with Hank. Perhaps his deductions weren't too far off. They were at least worth checking into. Where were Senator Buchanan and Hannah's mother nine months before Hannah's birth?

Chapter 10

Hannah sat at the helm of the truck, inching slowly across the pasture, following the tractor and baling machine. Her gaze strayed to the big mirror on the side where she could watch Taz bending to retrieve a rectangular bale and toss it like a toy up onto the stack.

As warm as the air was with the sun shining down on them during the morning, he hadn't shed his shirt. Sadly. Hannah would love to watch the way his muscles rippled as he worked bare-chested. But then, the man wasn't stupid. When working with hay, a person really needed long sleeves to protect his skin from the prickly straw.

They pushed through lunch without stopping. When Percy finished baling, he pitched in and helped load the final bales onto the truck and trailer.

Meanwhile, clouds had topped the peaks and rolled across the sky, blocking out all of the sunshine. They appeared heavy, laden with rain just waiting to fall.

Hannah drove the truck along the southern fence that served as the border between the Brighter Days ranch and the Rafter N Ranch owned by Will Nash.

The fence needed mending in several places and sagged in others. Hannah made a mental note to get out there when the weather was better and shore up the wire and nails.

Ever since Will Nash's open-heart surgery, his share of fence upkeep had fallen by the wayside. And Troy's heart didn't seem to be in ranching. For that matter, he didn't seem to be into anything having to do with work.

Hannah, being the person she was, gave the young man a chance when he responded to the ad she'd placed on the diner window for hired hands to help haul hay. From Percy's account, Troy wasn't much help. He loaded a single bale for every two Abe or Mark managed. She wouldn't hire him on for the task again. She needed men who worked hard. Men like Taz, who made hay-hauling look like child's play.

As she stared at the fence in a sad state of repair, a movement caught her eye on the other side.

A young heifer raced across a field, headed toward them. Behind her was a pack of timber wolves, gaining ground quickly. The lead wolf leaped up onto the back of the heifer and dragged her down.

Hannah slammed the truck into Park and jumped out. "Hey! Hey!" she shouted, running toward the fence. She braced her hand on a post, stepped up on a wire and launched herself over. Then she raced toward the downed heifer and the pack of wolves, her focus on saving the young cow.

Shouts rose behind her, but she didn't slow.

The heifer bawled, the anguished sound cutting straight to Hannah's heart. She had to get there before the wolves tore into her throat, severing her jugular vein.

Pulse pounding, lungs screaming, Hannah pressed on.

A shot rang out.

The majority of the wolves jumped and scattered. All except the one with his teeth sunk into the hindquarters of the bovine.

Hannah scooped up rocks and kept running, shouting, "Leave it alone! Go away! Shoo!" She flung the rocks at the wolves, but they weren't leaving their catch.

A force hit her from behind, sending her flying forward to land hard on her chest, the air jettisoning from her lungs.

Then a body climbed up hers and lay on top of her. "Stay down."

When she could get enough air past her vocal cords, she managed to wheeze, "But the cow—"

"Will be fine on her own," Taz's voice sounded against her ear. "The wolf let go. She's up and running."

"Then why are you still lying on top of me?"

"Someone was shooting a weapon."

"At the wolves, right?"

"We don't know. The shooter wasn't one of our group."

Hannah laid still, her gaze sweeping the nearby tree line, her heart still hammering. "No one's shooting now."

"I assume because they can't get a clear shot of you. Do you want to give them one?"

She shook her head. Hannah didn't want him to take a hit for her.

"Neither do I." He shifted, braced his hands on the ground and started to rise.

Another shot rang out. This one hit the dirt close to where Hannah and Taz lay.

Footsteps pounded across the hard-packed earth toward them.

Percy arrived, carrying a shotgun. He squatted, assuming a position on one side of Hannah.

Gavin joined them, and crouched next to her on the other side, aiming a rifle at the brush. "You all right, kid?"

"A little breathless, but I'm okay. How's the heifer?"

"She's long gone." Percy bent over and placed his hands on his knees, dragging in deep lungfuls of breath. "Don't ever take off after a pack of wolves again. That has to be the stupidest thing you've ever done." He pressed a hand to his chest, still breathing hard. "You like to gave me a heart attack."

She grimaced. "I'll admit, that wasn't my brightest move. But I couldn't let the wolves kill her."

Franklin, Vasquez and Young arrived a moment later.

"Holy shit, Miss Kendricks," Franklin said. "What were you trying to do, take on the entire wolf nation single-handedly?"

"We didn't see you take off until you leaped that fence like an Olympic hurdler," Vasquez said.

"What were you going to do if you got to the cow while those wolves were there?" Young asked.

"They'd have ripped you to shreds," Taz said, his voice shaking, his chest still heaving from running.

"I'll check the tree line," Gavin said. "Franklin, Vasquez, take my position here and guard Miss Kendricks."

"Yes, sir!" the two said and dropped down on one knee each beside Hannah and Taz.

Crouching low, Gavin took off at a run, zigzagging toward the tree line until he disappeared into the brush.

"Is he going to be okay?" Hannah asked.

"He's trained to do this kind of thing," Taz replied. "You can take the soldier out of the war, but you can't take away his training." His voice was terse, his body tense.

Hannah struggled to drag in a deep breath. "I think you can let me up. I'm pretty well covered by everyone."

"Let Blackstock check for the shooter. Then I'll consider letting you up."

"I can't breathe," she said on a desperate whisper.

Immediately, he eased up a little.

But his body still covered hers. If someone fired a shot at her, he'd take the hit.

Hannah didn't like the idea one bit. At the same time, her heart fluttered over his willingness to protect her no matter the cost. The man would give his life for her.

Hannah's chest swelled and warmth spread throughout her body.

A shout sounded from the direction Gavin had gone. A man emerged, being shoved forward by Gavin who had the man's arm twisted up behind his back with one hand, carrying a rifle in the other.

"I wasn't aiming at the woman. I was aiming at the wolves."

Anger surged. Hannah hadn't wanted to believe Troy could be the one targeting her. She'd hired the young man, giving him a chance to earn an honest wage, and this was what she got for her effort? "I believe you can let me up," Hannah said, ready to rip into her neighbor's son. "That's Troy Nash."

"Was he alone?" Taz called out.

"Ain't no one out here but me. And a good thing I was here, or those goddamn wolves would have finished off that heifer."

Gavin gave Troy one last shove before releasing him.

The young man came to a halt in front of the group from Brighter Days Ranch. He shook back his shoulders and lifted his chin. "And by the way, you're trespassing on Rafter N property."

Taz got up from the ground and helped Hannah to her feet.

She rose, dusted off her clothes and squared off with Troy. "Is that being neighborly, Troy? I chase off after a pack of wolves, trying to save one of your daddy's heifers, and that's all you have to say?"

Gavin closed in on Nash. "And what were you thinking firing at those wolves when you clearly had to have seen Hannah almost on them? You could have hit her."

"One of those rounds was six inches short of hitting her." Percy said.

Troy reached for his rifle. "That's mine."

"Give me all of your ammo, and I'll give you the rifle." Gavin pulled the bolt to the rear, ejecting the chambered round, and released the magazine. "And why are you carrying an AR15 semi-automatic? You starting a war out here?"

Troy crossed his arms over his chest. "I have a right to bear arms. It says so in the Constitution. And I only fired one round. Well above the heads of those wolves to scare them off. I didn't want to hit the heifer."

"There were two shots fired," Taz said.

"One of them kicked up dust in my face," Hannah said.

Troy shook his head. "Wasn't me. I got no beef with you or the Brighter Days Ranch. Why would I want to shoot you?"

"I don't know." Hannah stepped up to Troy. "You tell me. Have I done something to make you mad?"

The young man backed away, a flush starting

159

at his collar, working its way up through his cheeks and all the way out to the tips of his ears. "No. I don't guess you have."

Hannah held out her hand. "Gavin, give me his rifle."

Gavin handed the rifle to her.

She wanted to tear the young man apart, but knew it would do more damage than good. "I trust that if you did have a problem with me, you'd let me know and we could talk about it." She laid the rifle in his hands.

"I suppose," Troy said, taking the weapon. He glanced around at the people surrounding him. "I—I gotta get back to the house. The rain's about to start."

"That's a good idea," Hannah said. "And tell your daddy I said hello. He's a good man."

"I will." Troy cast another glance around the circle surrounding Hannah and then he turned and ran back to the brush Gavin had flushed him out of.

A moment later, Hannah could see him through the tree trunks and branches, riding off on a sorrel horse.

"Why would Troy lie about shooting multiple shots?" Gavin asked.

"Good question." Percy stepped up beside Hannah. "Are you all right?"

She nodded. "Why would Troy admit to shooting once, but not the second round?"

Gavin frowned down at Hannah. "Don't tell me you believed him?"

"None of us were carrying weapons," Franklin said. "They were all in the truck."

"And we wouldn't be shooting toward you, if we were," Vasquez added.

Hannah stared in the direction Troy had gone. "If he didn't shoot that second round, who did?" A chill swept down her spine as another thought occurred. "And since I was completely covered practically from head to toe, was he shooting at me or Taz?"

Taz held up his hands. "You're the one who was plagued by problems before I got here. Why would someone start shooting at me? I don't know anyone here."

Hannah shrugged. "I don't know. Just a thought." She glanced up at the clouds. They'd lowered to cover the higher peaks. "We'd better get going or the rain will start before we get the hay unloaded."

The group headed back for the fence and climbed over or through.

"And that's another job for another day." Hannah waved a hand at the sagging wires.

"Not today," Percy said.

"Right. We have to beat the rain to the barn."

The team strapped down the hay and climbed onto the bales stacked in the back of the truck. Soon the vehicles were bumping along the rutted path back to the barnyard.

When they reached the barn, Cookie was there, holding the gate open, waiting for them to pass through.

Cookie held up a hand.

Hannah slowed to a stop. "What's up?"

Cookie shot a glance toward the ranch house. "Holloway is at the house. He brought some woman along, and wants to see you."

Hannah's lips pressed into a line. "Tell him, if they want to see me, they can put on some work clothes and come help get this hay into the barn before it rains. Otherwise, they can wait until I'm done out here."

Cookie grinned. "I'll gladly pass on that message. Do you need my help?"

"Thanks, but no. We're going to be starving by the time we get done here. Which means having a meal ready is your top priority."

"Aye, aye!" Cookie snapped a salute and hurried toward the house.

"We can handle unloading the hay if you need to go," Gavin said.

"Holloway can wait." She shot a glance toward the heavy clouds lowering as she spoke. "Those rain clouds can't." Though her curiosity was piqued by Holloway's desire to see her immediately, and the woman he'd brought with him, Hannah wouldn't get sucked into whatever he wanted until the job was done.

They all worked together, unloading the hay into the barn, stacking it to the ceiling in the loft, leaving room for the next cutting. They'd need every bale to make it through the harsh winter.

Holloway managed the finances. He of all people had to understand the importance of

getting the hay stored before the rain.
No matter, they could wait.

Chapter 11

Taz worked beside Hannah, admiring her strength and determination.

When she'd gone after the wolves, he'd been just as surprised by her move as the others. He'd figured she had more sense. He hated to think what might have happened if he hadn't reached her before she got to the heifer. The potential results made his stomach churn still.

As they unloaded the last ten bales of hay, the skies opened up like giant faucets being turned on full blast.

Too tired to clean up first, they all slogged up to the house for dinner. They could shower and fall into their beds later.

Franklin and Vasquez gave Young a ride in the wheelbarrow to keep him from having to be elbow deep in the mud. For once, Young didn't argue.

Gavin offered to push the wheelbarrow, but the two one-armed men declined. They'd bonded with Young and made an odd but effective team.

When Hannah slipped in the mud, Taz was there, sliding an arm around her waist to steady her. She didn't push him aside or step free of his arm until they reached the house.

Hannah toed off her boots and stood them outside the back door.

Taz and the others followed suit. Everyone entered the kitchen in damp socks, dripping wet and grinning, satisfied with a day's hard work.

"I hope you're hungry," Cookie said. "I made up a double batch of hearty beef stew and enough bread rolls for you each to have as many as you can eat."

A cheer went up and they padded to the table.

Lori entered the room, smiling. "You all look like something the cat dragged in."

"Where were you?" Franklin asked. "We could have used another hand in the barn."

She waved her hand, her gesture encompassing the kitchen. "I was helping Cookie chop vegetables. He also taught me how to make to-die-for brownies."

Vasquez pressed his palms together. "Please tell me you made enough for everybody?"

She hesitated and then grinned. "We did."

Vasquez sighed. "I think I've died and gone to heaven."

As was the custom, the men waited for Hannah and Lori to take their seats before they scrambled into their own.

Taz pulled out Hannah's chair.

She took a step toward the table when a male voice spoke behind her. "Miss Kendricks?"

Taz spun to face the intruders.

A young man and an older woman entered the kitchen.

Hannah turned to give the young man a tight

smile. "Mr. Holloway. Would you and your guest care to join us?"

The young man started to say something, but the woman beside him wrinkled her nose and beat him to it.

"We most certainly would not. Do you not have a sense of decency? How can you come to the table covered in mud and smelling like the inside of a barn?"

Taz took a step forward, ready to tell the woman where she could go.

Hannah's hand shot out, stopping him. "My apologies if our bedraggled state offends you. We've been working hard and are tired and hungry." Hannah held out her hand. "I don't believe I've had the pleasure of meeting you. I'm Hannah Kendricks."

"I know who you are," the woman said, her nose still crinkling. She ignored Hannah's outstretched hand and pulled herself up to her full height of a few inches taller than Hannah. "I'm Charise Holloway Buchanan. My husband, Senator Buchanan, and I own this ranch. And you know my son, Martin."

Taz's respect for Hannah grew even broader as she stood straight and tall in front of the senator's wife.

"Nice to meet you. Please, wait in the living room. I'll be with you once I've had a chance to eat and take a shower. I shouldn't take more than twenty minutes."

The woman snorted. "I'd think you'd make it

quicker than that."

"Twenty minutes and I'll give you my undivided attention." Hannah shot the woman a tight-lipped smile, turned away and took her seat.

The others didn't hesitate, taking their cue from Hannah.

Taz waited until Mrs. Buchanan and her son left the kitchen. Then he sat beside Hannah. She sat stiff, waiting for those around her to help themselves to the bread rolls and butter. When the others had what they wanted, she smiled. "Thank you all for the tremendous amount of work you accomplished today. What you've done helps to ensure the horses have food for the winter."

Cookie ladled stew into their bowls and set the pot in the middle of the table before he, too, settled into a chair.

Taz ate two bowls of stew and three bread rolls. Beside him, Hannah picked at the excellent stew, pushing it around the bowl with her spoon. She ate a bite or two of a roll and set it aside. "Cookie and Lori, thank you for an outstanding meal. Now, if you'll excuse me, I need to take care of business." She pushed back her chair and left the room.

Taz finished the last bite of his roll and stood. "Good chow. Thanks. I'm calling it a night." He left the table and hurried to catch up to Hannah.

She was stepping out of her room with fresh clothes in hand.

"Are you all right?" he asked.

She nodded. "Knowing who owns the ranch feels weird. All this time, I thought it was some faceless organization. I can't believe a senator and his wife...." She stared up at him, her brow furrowed. "Why didn't he come out and tell us three years ago? Why all the secrecy? And why hasn't Martin said anything? Was he sent to spy on us?"

"Maybe the senator didn't want to make the rehab ranch a big media circus." Taz had really wanted to tell her earlier that he'd heard Senator Buchanan was behind the purchase of the ranch. But if he told her, she'd wonder where he'd gotten his information and why.

Taz had been hired to provide security for Hannah by an undisclosed individual. Before he knew Hannah, he didn't have a problem keeping secrets from her. The past couple days getting to know her had changed things.

Hannah was a good person with a heart of gold. She would never lie, and she'd expect no less from him. But he wasn't at liberty to tell her the truth. For now, he had to keep his secret, until such time he was relieved of his duties.

She stared up at him, her hair tangled with straw, her face streaked with dirt and her clothes wrinkled and filthy. Despite being scruffy dirty, she was still beautiful.

"I guess you're right. I should be glad we don't have a crowd of reporters descending on us every time we take a breath." She gave him a tired smile. "If you're waiting on me, I should be done in five minutes."

"Take your time," Taz said.

She snorted. "I'm already inconveniencing Mrs. Buchanan." She shook her head. "Who knew Holloway was a senator's son?"

"Stepson, by the sound of it."

"Still, he never let on whenever he was out here." She turned toward the bathroom, took a step and looked at him over her shoulder. "Thanks for protecting me this afternoon. I know what I did was foolish, but I couldn't let the heifer die."

"I understand. I'm just glad I was there to stop you when I did."

She gave him a real smile that warmed his insides. "Me, too." Hannah entered the bathroom and closed the door. A moment later Taz heard the water come on.

He could imagine her peeling the damp denim off her skin and stepping beneath the warm spray. How he would love to be in that shower with her. His groin tightened.

He drew in a deep breath and let it out slowly. Somehow, he needed to get word to Hank that the senator's cat was out of the bag and the folks at Brighter Days knew who had purchased the ranch.

Taz stood on the landing, overlooking the home's entrance. He wondered if the senator's ownership of the ranch meant anything to the investigation. Did Mrs. Buchanan or her son have a gripe against Hannah? Perhaps Hank, Bear or another of Patterson's operatives should visit with Troy and give him the right motivation to confess, if he was in any way responsible for tampering with the brakes on the tractor or the rail in the loft.

If Taz weren't charged with protecting Hannah, he'd interrogate Troy himself. But he wouldn't leave Hannah alone. Not with multiple attempts on her life, the latest being even more aggressive.

He wasn't certain how Mrs. Buchanan or Martin Holloway fit into the picture. He needed to let Patterson know they'd arrived.

While Hannah was in the shower, Taz listened at the top of the stairs for the sounds of people talking in the living room and the folks still working on their dinner. No one moved about the bottom of the staircase, and no sounds came from any of the rooms on the landing.

If there were a telephone on the second floor, it would be in Hannah's room and possibly one in the master bedroom.

With a quick glance around, he hurried toward Hannah's door, twisted the knob and breathed a quick sigh when it turned.

Feeling a twinge of guilt at invading her privacy without her permission, Taz entered, spied the telephone on the nightstand and went directly to it. Fishing Patterson's number out of his wallet, he lifted the phone from its cradle and listened. The dial tone buzzed in his ear. He quickly entered the numbers and waited while it rang on the other end.

Someone answered on the second ring. "Brotherhood Protectors. Hank speaking."

"Hey. We have visitors."

A brief pause followed. "Okay."

"Two. Senator's spouse and stepson."

"Gotcha. I guess his secret's not so secret anymore."

"Out here." Taz hung up and turned to leave. He hadn't taken a step when he stopped and stared at the woman in the doorway.

Her brow was marred by a fierce frown. "What the hell?" Hannah demanded.

A sharp stab of guilt hit him in the gut. Deciding to play innocent, he gave her an apologetic grin. "My cellphone had no reception. Since I needed to use the phone, I figured you would have one in your room. I didn't think you'd mind."

She crossed her arms over her chest. "Don't."

"Don't what?"

"I heard you telling someone we had visitors. Who were you calling?"

Crap. He wasn't getting out of this one easily. "A friend of mine."

"You'll have to do better than that."

Given the situation, and the intelligence of the woman standing in front of him, Taz opted for the truth. He strode toward her, captured her hand in his and tugged her all the way into the room, shutting the door behind her.

She remained stiff, her face set in stern lines. "I took self-defense. If you try anything, I'll take you down faster than you can feed me whatever lie you're about to tell me."

He pressed a finger to her lips. "Shh. I'll tell you the truth. But I prefer it remain between me and you."

She pushed aside his finger aside. "Why should I trust you?"

"Because I was sent to protect you."

Her brows rose. "To what?"

"I was hired to protect you."

"Like a bodyguard?" she asked.

He nodded.

Her eyes narrowed. "By whom?"

"I was hired by a man named Hank Patterson. He runs an organization called Brotherhood Protectors. His organization provides security services—"

"To the highest bidder?"

"To whomever needs them." Taz ran a hand through his hair. "Look, his business accomplishes two pretty great services. It provides jobs to guys like me who have been trained in combat, who might struggle to find employment in the civilian sector. In turn, he uses our skills to provide protection to people who need it most."

"Hank is Allie Patterson's older brother, isn't he?"

He shrugged. "I don't know. I'm new to the group. Hank assigned me to this gig right off the plane."

The tension left Hannah's shoulders and her lips thinned. "So, that's it? I'm a gig? A job you couldn't refuse?"

"No," he said, shaking his head. He reached for her hand, but she pulled back. "Well, yes. But I took the job because I needed it."

"Which means you didn't come to the ranch for therapy and rehabilitation, did you?" Her jaw tightened. "What else did you lie about?"

He looked away. "Hank chose me because, of all his employees, I was most recently released from the service and Walter Reed. Everything I told you about my injuries is true. I was diagnosed with TBI. I have difficulties controlling my anger, and I have situational memory loss."

"And you expect me to take your word for it?"

"You can look at my medical records, if it would make you feel better. Hank had them sent to the ranch. Do whatever it takes. The important issue here is that you have been targeted on multiple occasions. Until we determine who did the targeting, we have to assume you're still in danger. I'm here to protect you."

"So all of that protection crap you fed me earlier was just you doing your job." She jerked her head toward the door. "Get out of my room."

"Are you going to let me continue to perform my assignment?" he asked, afraid she'd send him packing and kick him off the ranch.

"I would be the last person to get a man

fired. Especially since you're doing such a good job at it." Her tone dripped sarcasm. "And I'm sure you only kissed me to keep me close and make your mission easier. I get that. Just don't do it again. Stay out of my way and don't...touch me again. Now, if you'll excuse me, I have to deal with the owner of this ranch."

He nodded. Though his heart pinched tight in his chest. He hated seeing the disappointment in her eyes. Not wanting to push her any more than he had, he let her believe what she did. Perhaps doing so was better than letting her know the truth.

Besides, one of the owners of the ranch was waiting downstairs waiting for her. Hannah had her own job to do, and Taz didn't want to get in the way. But he sure as hell would be close by to make sure Mrs. Buchanan and Martin Holloway weren't part of Hannah's problem.

He'd find a way to make it up to Hannah. She deserved the truth. And the truth was he'd kissed her because he'd wanted to, not to get closer to make his job easier. In fact, kissing her made his job so much more difficult.

Chapter 12

Hannah thought about wearing a dress and nice shoes for her meeting with the lady who owned the ranch, but she'd already made a bad impression. She might as well be dressed in comfy clothing for what was sure to be an uncomfortable meeting.

When she stepped into the living room, her hackles rose and her fists clenched.

Charise Holloway Buchanan stood by the fireplace, holding the picture of Hannah and her mother when Hannah was only six.

Hannah resisted marching across the room and yanking the frame from the woman's hands. "Mrs. Buchanan, Martin, perhaps you'd like to take a seat?"

The woman glanced up from her perusal of the photo. "Is this you and your daughter?"

Anyone who had known Hannah's mother remarked on how much Hannah looked like her. "No, ma'am, that's me and my mother, when I was a child."

Mrs. Buchanan glanced back at the photo, her eyes narrowing. Finally, she set the frame back on the mantel, it face down.

Hannah's hackles rose. She strode across the room, set the frame upright, adjusted it to the previous angle and faced Mrs. Buchanan. "How can I help you?"

Mrs. Buchanan drew herself to her full height, standing a good three inches taller than Hannah. "I came to see what exactly is going on with our investment."

Hannah nodded, preferring to stand as long as the other woman did the same. "We're doing what the investment group asked me to do. We're working with wounded veterans to help them regain their confidence and independence."

"And how can that happen? From what I observed of the veterans who came in from the fields, some of them are missing limbs." Her brows rose. "How are they supposed to regain their independence? What good are they on a ranch like this? Surely the work is far too hard for them to accomplish without help."

Hannah's fists clenched. She shot a glance toward Martin, the woman's son. He stood at the far side of the room, his face pinched, his hands dug into his pockets. Hadn't he told his mother about the program? Wasn't he here often enough to see for himself the good they accomplished?

Lifting her chin and squaring her shoulders, she faced Mrs. Buchanan. "Our clients come to the ranch after trying to fit in back home and failing miserably. When they arrive here, they're depressed and close to defeat. We put them to work helping rescued horses. Working with the animals, they aren't judged, and they aren't laughed at. They have time to learn just how much they can do without the assistance of others. The veterans learn they have value."

"And who but the horses know this? Really, Miss Kendricks, I hardly see how this is helping anyone. All I see is my husband's hard-earned money being thrown into a bottomless pit."

Hannah's teeth clenched. She wanted to fly at the woman, scratch her eyes out and call her a bitch. For the sake of the program and the people and horses who benefited from it, she held back her inner mama bear and gave a stiff nod. "I'm sorry you feel that way."

"Not only are you wasting money on these men, who should be in the care of occupational therapists, you're throwing good money after bad on animals that would be better off euthanized." She advanced on Hannah. "Aren't you ashamed of yourself for drawing a paycheck for this sham of an operation? When I get back to Bozeman, I'll have words with my husband."

Standing straight, Hannah faced the woman refusing to back down. "When I was tasked with this concept, I was given carte blanche to set up the program any way I saw fit. The wounded warriors were the primary focus and still are. As far as I'm concerned, I'm accomplishing what I set out to do."

"And she's doing a damned fine job of it," a voice said behind her.

Hannah spun to find Taz standing in the doorway to the living room.

His gaze leveled on Mrs. Buchanan, his jaw tight and his fists clenched. "The men and women respect her and do what she says, because they see the benefit to themselves and the animals they learn to care for."

Mrs. Buchanan's nose wrinkled. "And who are you?"

"One of the men Miss Kendricks is working with. She's done incredible work with her clients. They're happy, healthy and learning they can be successfully independent."

At his praise, Hannah's chest swelled.

The woman snorted, her gaze raking over him from head to toe. "I don't see how *you* need help."

Hannah's claws came out. The woman could attack *her* all day, but she had no business directly attacking a client. "Ma'am, you might own the ranch, but I won't have my clients treated badly. Mr. Davila, like many of the men and women who come here, nearly died in battle defending this great country you have the privilege to live in. He deserves your respect, not your judgment. Not all injuries are easy to see." Hannah stood with her shoulders back, her head held high. No one mistreated her clients.

Taz laid a hand on her shoulder. "What Miss Kendricks is telling you is that what happens here is legit and highly beneficial to the veterans who participate in the program."

Although she was still angry with him for his lies, Hannah felt comforted by his presence and grateful that in such a short time, Taz had witnessed the benefits the clients gained from being there.

Mrs. Buchanan glanced at the photograph on the mantel, her lips pressed into a tight line. "Well, we'll see. I'll return tomorrow to inspect the premises." She swung her gaze back to Hannah. "I'm not convinced you're the right person for this job."

The woman's words stabbed Hannah in the gut. "If you feel that way, why was I specifically asked to get this operation rolling?"

"I don't know. But I certainly intend to find out." She turned to Martin. "Are you ready?"

As much as she hated posing the question, Hannah asked, "Will you and Mr. Holloway be staying here tonight?"

Mrs. Buchanan wrinkled her nose. "Certainly not." She waved her hand at Holloway. "Come, Martin."

"I'll be right there," Martin said. "I need to get something from my office."

The woman left the room without responding and sailed through the front door, shutting it with a bang.

Holloway stopped in front of Hannah and said in a low voice, "I'm sorry for the unexpected visit. My mother isn't normally so unkind. And she's wrong. What you're doing here is amazing."

Hannah warmed to his compliment and touched his arm. "Thank you, Martin."

The young man left.

For a long moment, Hannah stood, staring at the photo of her and her mother. Life seemed so much simpler then.

"Are you all right?" Taz asked.

She nodded and turned. "I'm hitting the sack. Tomorrow will come soon enough." Hannah paused as she passed Taz on her way out. "Thanks for sticking up for me. You didn't have to."

"I only spoke the truth." He raised his hand toward her face, stopping before he actually touched her. "You are doing a great job with the people and horses in your care."

"Not according to Mrs. Buchanan."

Taz snorted. "She doesn't know what she's talking about."

"Well, thanks." Reminding herself she was still angry with Taz, Hannah climbed the stairs and entered her room, locking the door behind her. Stripping out of her clothes, she pulled a T-shirt over her head. Her body dragged with exhaustion, but her mind spun through everything that had happened that day.

Footsteps sounded on the landing. They entered the room beside hers and the door clicked shut.

Hannah lay in her bed on the other side of the wall from Taz, wanting to hate him, but having a very hard time with the emotion.

She was mad that he had lied about why he was there. Mad because he could have been cozying up just to protect her. The kisses...they weren't real. They couldn't be. She was just a job to him. Nothing more.

Or was she?

She rolled over on her stomach and pounded her pillow. Why couldn't people be honest and true? Both the senator and Taz had lied. Apparently, she was gullible. She wondered who else had lied she didn't know about. And why did someone want to hurt her? She wasn't anybody but a therapist working to do good for the veterans who had sacrificed so much to protect the country.

She lay for a long time with her face buried in the pillow, thinking she could stay that way and suffocate. Just finish what someone else had started and be done with it.

Soon, her need for air and her desire to live made her lift her head and take a deep breath. Sleep was the farthest thing from her mind. Lying in bed wouldn't get her there, so she got up, threw on a robe and tiptoed downstairs.

Lori had taken the puppy to her room that night. The living room and kitchen were empty.

Hannah hesitated at the front door. After the attempts on her life, she should be worried about walking outside without her bodyguard.

But the walls seemed to close in on her. She needed to get out. She unlocked the front door and walked out onto the porch, breathing in the cool mountain air. No matter how sad, worried or upset she was, a deep breath of Montana air always calmed her and made things right with her world.

She waited for the calm to wash over her, but

her pulse still pounded, her chest remained tight and she couldn't stop the thoughts whirling around in her head. She should tell Taz she had left the house, having promised she would. But she couldn't. He was the biggest reason she couldn't sleep.

Keeping an eye on the yard bathed in moonlight, Hannah hugged the shadows of the porch and paced from one end of the house to the other, going over all that had happened in the past few days. Her thoughts kept returning to the man upstairs in the bedroom beside hers.

Taz. Appropriately nicknamed. He'd spun into Hannah's life, stirred it up and, as soon as they figured out the mystery saboteur, Taz would spin right back out. In his wake, he'd leave a confused and sad woman who would always wonder if there could have been more between them, had they been give more time together.

Surely the kisses had meant more than just part of the lie. Perhaps if they'd done more than kiss, she wouldn't be so wound up about the man. Maybe the chemistry she'd felt in his arms wouldn't translate into bed.

And pigs might still learn to fly.

Who was she kidding? A man like Taz had to be incredible in bed. And Hannah would never know just how incredible.

She stood with her back to the house and sucked in several deep, calming breaths. Tonight they did nothing to soothe her soul. Finally, she spun and smacked into a hard wall of muscles.

Startled, she opened her mouth to scream.

An arm wrapped around her waist, a hand clamped over her lips and a face swam in front of hers. "It's me, Taz."

The fear left her body, replaced by an entirely different form of tension.

Sexual, sensual desire coiled around her core, spreading heat so hot it threatened to undermine her control over her senses.

Taz lowered his hand, his gaze hard on her face. "You promised you wouldn't go anywhere without me."

"I didn't. I'm still here at the ranch house," she said, her voice breathy, her skin tingling in every spot he touched her.

"Anywhere outside the house could be dangerous. Even inside the house. With as many people coming and going, someone could leave a door or window unlocked. Your attacker could get in and do you harm." He smoothed the hair off her cheek and tucked a strand behind her ear. "Please. Let me know when you're going somewhere." He cupped her cheek in his hand.

"I needed time alone to think." She leaned into his palm, incapable of resisting her need to feel his skin against hers. *Sweet Jesus.* She wanted him. But he wasn't here as her lover. He was her bodyguard. "Away from—"

"Away from me?" He wrapped his arms around her waist and pressed her against him.

He wore jeans and nothing else. A hard ridge nudged her belly, making her aware he wasn't immune. Based on the length and thickness of his erection, he was just as turned on by her as she was by him.

She rested her cheek on his bare chest and listened to the sound of his racing heartbeat. Her own heart filled with joy and hope.

Taz brushed his lips across her temple, the heat of his breath warming her skin. "Maybe you're right. When you're near, I can't think straight. How can I protect you, when all I want is to hold you in my arms, kiss you and make love to you?"

She chuckled softly, her fingers curling into his skin, scraping against his muscles. "I'm not stopping you." God, he was built like a brick wall, a man trained to kill. Yet, he could be tender and caring and his kisses...

Her knees threatened to buckle and her woman parts melted, creaming at the thought of what his hardened shaft would feel like inside her.

"This is so wrong," he said as he swept her off her feet and into his arms.

"In so many ways," she agreed, hiding a smile as she slipped her arm around his shoulder.

"But I can't stop myself."

She weaved her hands into the hair at the back of his head and pulled his mouth down to meet hers. "Then don't stop." And she kissed him.

He opened to her and she swept her tongue past his teeth to duel with his in a sensuous dance.

For a long moment he held her there,

suspended in his arms, her feet high above the floor.

The kiss seemed to last forever, yet ended too soon.

Taz spun, pushed through the front door and turned long enough to let her close and lock the deadbolt.

Then he was striding across the floor and up the stairs. He didn't stop until he'd cleared the door to his bedroom, entering like a conquering hero.

Hannah wanted to laugh out loud. Her heart beat so fast she felt as if it might fly out of her chest. And the ache between her legs was so profound, she might die if he didn't come inside her soon. Then a thought pierced the rush of her fantasy, bringing her back to Earth for an abrupt moment. "Protection?"

He laid her on the bed and bent over her to press a quick kiss to her lips. "Got it." Taz reached for his wallet on the nightstand, producing two foil packages.

"My hero." She wrapped her arms around his neck, pulling him down on top of her.

He lay there for a moment, exploring her mouth, feasting on her lips, and then pushed up straightened arms. "This isn't going to work," he said, breathing hard.

She frowned. "What do you mean?" Her spirits sank, forming a hollow in her belly.

He smiled. "How can I make love to you when we're both fully dressed?"

Hannah felt her lips part in a wide grin. "I can fix that." She sat up, untied the belt on her robe and yanked her arms free. Then she reached for the hem of her shirt and dragged it up her torso.

Taz stilled her movement with one hand and shook his head. "Let me."

She relinquished her hold on the hem and stared up into his eyes as he slowly lifted her shirt. His dark-eyed gaze followed the path of the garment, devouring every inch of skin revealed along the way.

Cool air caressed her naked breasts, and then his tongue flicked the tip of one.

Hannah sucked in a swift breath and arched her back, urging Taz to take more.

And he did. Laving, licking and nibbling on the turgid peak until he had Hannah gasping, her body on fire and ready for so much more.

The shirt flew off, landing somewhere on the other side of the room. Hannah didn't care where it went. Her focus was on getting him out of his jeans.

She reached for the hard metal button and pushed it open. As she slid the zipper downward, she captured his gaze and held it.

Nothing in her life felt more right than being naked with this man she barely knew.

His cock sprang free, straight, thick and full.

Hannah gasped, her pussy clenched and a rush of juices prepared her for his entry.

Taz hooked the elastic waistband of her

panties and dragged them down her legs. He pressed a kiss to the fluff of curls covering her sex and slid his lips along the inside of her thighs, kissing and nipping her as he tugged her panties to her ankles. They joined her shirt somewhere on the floor.

Hannah drew up her legs and let her knees fall to the side, opening herself to him.

Taz slipped between. With the tip of his finger, he traced a feathery line from the back of her knee upward, as if writing a poem or composing a symphony with her nerves.

She moaned and writhed, becoming impatient for what would come next. She wanted him. Inside her, filling her, stretching her channel until she couldn't tell where he ended and she began. "Now," she begged.

He chuckled, his breath stirring the hairs over her sex. "Not until you're ready."

"I'm ready," she said, finding it hard to talk, unable to catch a full breath between his nibbles and licks.

Then he parted her folds with his thumbs and blew a warm stream of air over her heated flesh.

"Oh, sweet Jesus," she whimpered. "Please."

"You're getting there." He flicked his tongue over her clit.

His touch set every nerve on fire. She reached down, weaving her fingers into his hair and dug them into his scalp. "I can't take much more," she whispered.

"Hold on tight, darlin', I've only just begun." Then he swept his tongue across her again, on this pass taking his time, licking, swirling and teasing.

Hannah arched her back off the bed, her breath locked in her lungs, every muscle tense. Waiting…waiting…

Taz pressed a finger to her entrance and slipped inside her warm wetness. He followed that one with two more digits, simultaneously intensifying his tongue assault.

She exploded in a fiery burst, tingling bolts of electricity rippling from her core outward to the very tips of her fingers and toes. She flung back her head and cried out, "Taz, oh, dear, sweet heaven. I'm coming apart."

He laughed and tongued her again, sustaining his attack until she collapsed back to the bed.

"Now you're ready." He climbed up her body. Leaning over her, he gazed into her eyes.

Finally able to draw air into her lungs, she filled them and lay still while the aftershocks rippled through her. She clung to the sensations, knowing she hadn't yet experienced the full gambit of Taz's lovemaking prowess. Anxious for more, she held out a hand.

He pressed the foil packet into her palm and rose onto his knees.

Hannah tore it open, extracted the condom and slipped it over his throbbing shaft, all the way to the base. Unable to resist, she rolled his balls in her hands, all the while watching his expression tighten.

He sucked in a breath, his chest expanding.

She liked that she could control his reactions as well as he'd controlled hers. Then she wrapped both hands over his cock, warming it between her fingers. *Sweet Jesus.* The man was thick, hard and big enough to frighten a virgin.

Thankfully, she wasn't a virgin. But that didn't mean she was experienced. Her few forays into sex had been as a fumbling college student. Those events had ended in breaking off contact with the boy, because she was too embarrassed by her lack of knowledge on the subject. Being honest with herself, she really hadn't cared to repeat the awkward exchange.

With Taz, she felt natural, sexy and ready to give as good as she took. Tugging gently, she guided him to her center, lying back on the comforter as he nudged her damp entrance.

Taz leaned above her, his lips hovering over hers. "Kiss me," he commanded.

She lifted her head, meeting his mouth as he lowered it to hers. His tongue slipped past her teeth as he thrust inside her.

Her slick channel eased his entrance, allowing her to take all he had to give. The deeper he slid, the more complete she felt.

This sensation was what the movies, the books and the magazines were talking about. Hannah would gladly stay like this forever.

If only…

Chapter 13

Taz fought his desire to take this woman in hard, swift strokes. He sensed she needed to ease into their connection. If he moved too fast, he might scare her off. Cloaked in her tightness, he didn't want to leave her. But the natural urge to thrust and thrust again threatened to overtake his ability to take it slow.

When she wrapped her hands around his hips and pushed him back, he thought he might be hurting her. He knew he was big. And to a woman whose pussy was so snug, the distinct possibility existed she could be in pain. He prayed it wasn't so, but he had to respect her body.

Then she dug her fingers into his skin and slammed him back into her. "Faster," she said on a breathy sigh. "Can you go faster?"

He laughed, the tension releasing. "Oh, darlin', can I go faster." He set a slow, steady pace to start and quickly increased his speed until he was rocking in and out of her like a piston in a high-powered racing engine.

She dug her heels into the mattress and lifted her bottom off the bed, meeting each thrust with one of her own.

Sensations built, electricity sizzled and exploded inside Taz, jettisoning him over the edge. Slamming into her one last time, he buried himself deep inside and dropped down to press his chest against her naked breasts, holding her tight while his dick throbbed on.

When at last he came back to his senses, Taz realized he must have been crushing her. He rolled to his side, bringing her with him, retaining their intimate connection.

Hannah laid her head in the crook of his arm, one hand resting on his chest. "Wow."

A chuckle rose in Taz's throat. "I agree. Wow."

"I didn't know it could be so…so…"

"Intense?"

"Yes!" She snuggled closer, pressing her lips to his skin.

He raised his brows. "Your first orgasm?"

She gave a little shrug. "First not self-induced by my battery-operated boyfriend."

His heart skipped several beats. Strong, smart and sexy…and not averse to sex toys. He could well be in love. "You'll have to introduce us."

"Mmm. Someday. If you're still around," she mumbled, her voice trailing off. Soon her breathing deepened, and she slept

Taz disposed of the condom and then lay awake for a long time, reveling in the warmth of Hannah's body, memorizing every curve and nuance. He was almost afraid to go to sleep. What if he awoke and this had all been a dream?

Exhaustion claimed him in the early hours of the morning. The sleep he needed came with the hazy dreams he welcomed and dreaded at the same time. Perhaps this time he'd learn something.

Back in the Afghan village, his battle buddies at his side, he had a chance to do the mission all over again. A chance to get the procedure right, and bring his comrades home alive. But, no matter what he did, he couldn't change the course of events. He yelled at himself, "It's a trap! Don't open that door!" But his dream self didn't listen. The door opened, a face swam into view and he could swear he recognized it. Then the image was gone.

No!

He had to see, to know who was responsible for the grenade that ended his career and the lives of his teammates. But he lay on the ground, buried in debris, darkness and dust choking him.

"Taz," a soft voice called out, dragging him to the surface.

He coughed, amazed his lungs weren't filled with suffocating dust.

"Taz, open your eyes. You're dreaming." A gentle hand cupped his cheek and turned his head.

When he opened his eyes, he was staring into the face of an angel. "Am I dead?" he asked.

The angel laughed. "Hardly. You had a bad dream." She leaned up on one arm and pressed a kiss to his lips, her bare breasts brushing across his chest. "Wake up."

In an instant, he knew where he was, and the angel's name. "Hannah." Then he flipped over, taking her with him, pinning her back to the mattress, holding her hands above her head. "I could easily become obsessed with your body."

She laughed and moved her hips beneath him. "I get that, and ditto."

Instantly erect, he nudged her belly, his desire flaming inside.

Hannah was a distraction from his nightmare, from his job and from his memories. She was a distraction he couldn't afford, but couldn't find the strength to resist.

Starting at her forehead, he pressed kisses to her sweet-smelling skin, feathering his lips over her eyelids, across her cheekbones and down to claim her mouth in a long, soul-stealing connection of twisting tongues and raspy moans.

She was amazing, both heart and mind. Her inner strength shone through in her work with the veterans and her love of the animals.

Hannah could be everything Taz wanted and needed, but could he give the same in return? He pushed aside the question and made his absolute goal to pleasure her in every sexual way possible. If he couldn't be what she needed, he could at least make the time they had together unforgettable.

Once he ravaged her mouth completely, he worked his way down the side of her neck and over the swell of her breasts, treating each beaded nipple to a thorough tongue-teasing and gentle suction.

She dug her fingers into his hair and rocked her body against his. "Please, you're making me crazy."

He laughed softly, blowing a warm stream of air across her damp nipples. "Please what?"

"Please take me." She tipped up his head and gazed into his eyes. "Fill me. Come inside me, where you belong," she whispered. "Now."

He grabbed for the last of his condoms on the nightstand, handed it to her and came up on his knees.

Once she fitted it over his shaft, she lay back and spread her legs wide.

His pulse hammered hard in his veins, urging him to take what she offered. But he couldn't. Not until he had her so wet and aching she couldn't think straight

She reached for his hips.

He scooted backward. "Uh-uh."

"What do you mean, uh-uh?" she asked, her brows dimpling. "You can't stop now. That would be mean."

"I have no intention of stopping." He captured her mouth once more in a brief kiss, and then flipped her on her stomach and started his campaign at the back of her neck. Moving aside her long blond hair, he kissed, tongued and nipped the curve of her neck, the swells of her shoulders and along her spine to the crease down the middle of her sexy ass.

Then he lifted her hips and spread her knees, the better to lick the insides of her thighs.

Hannah arched her back, raising up her head to moan softly.

Taz slid a finger into her pussy and swirled it

around, coating his finger with her juices. Then he cupped her sex and slipped his wet finger between her folds, finding and stroking her clit until she covered his hand with hers and rocked back against him.

He bent to taste her, to stroke her with his tongue and press inside her to test just how close she was to coming. And boy was she wet, hot and ready.

Hannah gripped the comforter in her fingers. "Please. Don't make me wait. I have to have you. Inside. Me. Now."

He couldn't wait any longer. Her sweet, sexy ass beckoned him, her glistening pussy all the assurance he needed to know she wanted him as badly.

Cloaked and ready, he gripped her hips and thrust inside, burying himself so deeply he became one with her. Then he pulled out and thrust again, and again, rocking her and the bed so hard the headboard hit the wall, making enough noise to wake the household.

Easing back and restraining himself a little, he settled into a gentler, steady rhythm. As he pumped in and out of her, he bent over her back, reached around her belly for her clit and stroked her there.

The tension inside him mounted, sending him into the stratosphere. He flicked and stroked Hannah until her body stiffened and she drew in a deep breath. She held it for a long time, quivering beneath him, her climax every bit as powerful as his.

When she stopped trembling, he eased her to her belly and rolled them to their sides, pulling her back against his chest, his arm around her middle, holding on tight.

The sun was coming up, the pale light finding its way around the blinds. The others would be up soon. They'd have to get on with their lives and the work they were at Brighter Days to accomplish. Somehow, Taz wanted to capture the moment, to tuck it away and keep the memory forever.

"Hannah?" he said.

"Mmm?" She wiggled her bottom closer.

"What if I wasn't your bodyguard?" He drummed up the courage, knowing she could do so much better. "Would you go out with me?"

"On a real date?" she asked.

"Yeah." He went on before he could talk himself out of it. "I might not be the right guy for you, and I was discharged from the army due to TBI, so no guarantees on my health…" His arm tightened. "But would you consider going out with a broken-down soldier?"

Hannah frowned. "You're not broken." She smoothed a hand along the side of his cheek. "You went through something traumatic. Your mind is protecting you from your memories. You just have to relax and quit trying so hard to remember. When you do, your memories might come back on their own."

"Sweetheart, I think you're right." The more

he tried to force the images to appear, the foggier they became. He had to let go. "But, you didn't answer my question. Would go out with me?"

Hannah turned in his arms and opened her mouth to answer.

A loud knocking sounded from downstairs.

Hannah sat up. "What the hell?"

"Someone's knocking on the door." Taz rolled out of the bed and shoved his legs into his jeans. He collected Hannah's clothes and tossed them her way before dragging a T-shirt over his head.

Dressing almost as quickly, Hannah beat him to the door and stepped out.

Lori emerged from her room, rubbing her eyes. "What's going on?"

"I don't know." Hannah headed for the stairs.

Protective instincts surged. Taz grabbed her arms and pushed her behind him. "Let me go first."

She didn't argue, but followed on his heels down the stairs.

Percy reached the front hallway first. He peered through the side transoms and frowned. Then he unlocked and opened the door.

Holloway, his mother and a man dressed in a business suit stood on the porch.

The man in the suit stepped forward. "You must be Percy." He held out his hand. "James Buchanan."

"The senator?" Percy asked.

Buchanan nodded, his gaze going past Percy, past Taz and to the base of the stairs where Hannah stood. "I've come to see my daughter. Miss Hannah Kendricks.

Chapter 14

Hannah froze, her pulse racing. She stared at the man standing in the doorway. "What did you say?"

He grimaced and took a step toward her. "I came to see you. I know now, I shouldn't have waited so long to meet you." Senator James Buchanan, a man Hannah had only seen before on the television, walked toward her.

"This is ridiculous. How can she be your daughter if you've never even met?" Mrs. Buchanan from behind him.

"I knew her mother," he replied without taking his gaze off Hannah. "She looks just like Donna did all those years ago." He held out his hand. "I'm so sorry for your loss. When I knew her, she was a happy, vibrant woman with so much life in her."

"She was, even up to the day she died," Hannah whispered, having difficulty grasping the senator's words. "But she never said anything about my father. Until I got the letter from the lawyer. Even then, she didn't mention a name, only that she'd told him about me."

Mrs. Buchanan laid her hand on her husband's arm. "How do you know Miss Kendrick's mother wasn't lying about her daughter's paternity?"

"She sent me a lock of your hair, along with her letter." Senator Buchanan shoved a hand through his salt-and-pepper gray hair. He captured her gaze. "I sent it in with my own DNA sample. While I waited for the results, I hired a private investigator." He raised his hand. "I...needed...to know where Donna had been for the past nearly thirty years. I wanted to know who you were. What you were like."

"You had me followed?" Hannah shivered.

"I'm sorry to say, yes. I didn't want to believe the letter Donna sent. But I couldn't ignore it, either. And I couldn't wait for the results of the DNA test." Shaking his head, he sighed. "Put yourself in my shoes. What would you have done if you found out you had a twenty-seven-year-old daughter you never knew existed?"

Hannah stared at the man who suddenly appeared to grow older before her eyes. She searched his face, trying to see any resemblance between him and herself.

"I found out you'd been raised on this ranch, and that you considered it home for all those years. Then the results came back."

His wife's hand tightened on his arm and her eyes filled. "You never told me. I had to find out for myself."

"How could I? I was in the middle of a brutal re-election campaign when the news came through. You were suffering from depression." Glancing to the side, he patted his wife's hand. "I didn't even know what to do. Because, you see, our DNA matched." He scrubbed a hand down his face, and his voice cracked as he said, "Suddenly, I had a daughter."

Hannah's chest compressed so tightly she thought her lungs would implode.

Taz slipped an arm around her.

His touch provided warmth that couldn't begin to take away the chill sliding across Hannah's body.

"You knew for three years, but you didn't come to see the ranch—to see me." She waved hear hand wide, encompassing all she'd built, all she'd worked so hard to create. "Then why am I here? Why bring me back to this ranch?"

"The private investigator laid out the owner's circumstances, and I didn't want you to lose your home." Buchanan swallowed hard.

"So, you bought the ranch to keep me from leaving Montana?" She felt so betrayed, her eyes filled with tears she refused to let fall.

Taz's arm tightened, bringing her body closer to his.

The senator nodded. "You were going to leave to work at Walter Reed, halfway across the country. I had to do something to keep you here until...until." He stopped and shook his head.

"Until my mother got better." Martin Holloway stepped forward.

"I wasn't sick." Mrs. Buchanan shook her head. "You thought I was, but I wasn't."

"Mother, please," her son said. "You were falling apart. You threatened to commit suicide so often that, when you finally took an overdose of sleeping pills, you almost died because no one thought the attempt was real."

"You shouldn't have stopped me," Charise said and burst into tears. "You shouldn't have stopped me."

Hannah could hear the pain in Mrs. Buchanan's cry and her heart squeezed.

Martin slipped an arm around her shoulder. "You weren't well, mother. No one blames you."

"Oh, but you will. Everyone will." She slid to the floor, taking down her son, too.

He knelt beside her, stroking her back. "What do you mean? Why do you say we will blame you?"

She grabbed her son's collar and sobbed, "I did it to protect you. I swear I did it out of love for my son. You deserved to be the senator's child. Not some obscure bastard from a fling so long ago, no one would remember." She shook her son, her face ravaged by her tears, her makeup running in dark rivulets down her cheeks.

"Mother," Martin said, his voice stern, as he held her arm's length. "What did you do?"

Hannah's gut clenched as she stared at the woman who was her stepmother.

Charise turned to the senator. "You should have let her leave. You should have let her go on believing she didn't have a father."

"Charise." The senator's tone was low, commanding. "Explain yourself."

"I did what any mother would for her son. I

paid someone to get rid of the bitch."

"You paid—" Taz pushed Hannah behind him, using his body as a shield.

Hannah felt dizzy and her stomach bunched into a knot. She pressed a hand to her chest. How could this happen?

"Charise!" Senator Buchanan's voice barked loud, filling the room. "Who did you pay?"

"What does it matter? He failed miserably." Charise flung her hand toward Hannah. "She's still here, isn't she?"

Holloway took the woman's hands. "Mother, who did you pay?"

The senator's wife stared into Martin's eyes. "Some local kid who'd just lost his job. He needed money." She buried her face against her son's hands. "I needed her gone."

"What was his name, Mother?" Martin persisted.

"I don't know. Tray something? I didn't care. He knew who the Kendricks woman was. He promised to scare her off. Then he took the money and that was the last I saw of him."

"How much did you give him?" Senator Buchanan demanded.

"Ten thousand dollars." She snorted. "Apparently, ten thousand doesn't go as far as it used to." She turned her tear-ravaged face toward Hannah. "I should have hired a real hit man. I could have, you know." She lifted her chin and looked down her nose. "My family has connections."

"Charise!" Senator Buchanan shut her down with that one word.

She stared up at him, her eyes running over with tears. "Our marriage is over, isn't it?"

The senator's face was a grim, tight mask. "We'll discuss it later. The main thing is to stop this man from completing his task." He turned to Hannah and Taz. "Do you have any idea who she's talking about?"

Hannah nodded. "Troy Nash."

"Was that who you talked to?" Martin tipped up his mother's face.

"Yes, yes, that's him," Mrs. Buchanan said.

Her chest hurting, Hannah turned to Percy.

The foreman nodded. "I'll call his father."

"Follow up with a call to the sheriff," Taz recommended.

"Will do," Percy stepped into the hallway.

"In the meantime, what should I do?" Hannah asked, feeling as if her world was spinning out of control.

"Stay put until the boy is found," Taz said.

"Stay close to your bodyguard," the senator said. "I was told he'd be highly trained. The best of the best." His gaze cut to Taz. "That's you, isn't it?"

Taz nodded, his lips tight.

Hannah stared numbly at the man who'd just admitted he was her father. "You were the undisclosed client who hired Taz to protect me?"

He nodded, his gaze shifting to Holloway. "When Martin told me what happened with the tractor, I knew I had to do something, and fast. I thought one of my enemies had found out you were my daughter. I never suspected that enemy was my own wife."

"My son was supposed to inherit your legacy. Not the product of a fling with a whore!"

"Enough!" Senator Buchanan's shout all but raised the roof.

Mrs. Buchanan burst into more tears.

Though the woman's comment angered her, Hannah knew her mother wasn't a whore. Her gaze shifted to the photo on the mantel. Her mother had been a young woman who'd followed her heart and her hormones, making a mistake that affected the rest of her life. But she'd chosen not to give up on her child. She'd become a beautiful and loving mother.

Hannah stared down at Mrs. Buchanan, a woman who had, in her own twisted way, tried to protect her son and his future. She couldn't be too angry with her. As her son had said, she was sick. Mentally ill. She needed help.

With each thought passing trough her mind, Hannah's heartbeat skipped and raced ahead. One thought emerged on top. She had a father. "Where do we go from here?"

"You aren't going anywhere," Percy said from behind her.

Hannah spun. "Did you get Mr. Nash?"

"I spoke with Troy's father. He said Troy left the house early this morning." Percy's jaw hardened. "He told his father he had a job he was working."

"What did the sheriff say?" Taz asked.

"He put out a call to his units to be on the lookout for Nash. If they find him, they'll bring him in for questioning."

A door at the back of the house crashed open, making Hannah jump.

"Hannah! Percy! Where is everyone?" Lori called out, followed by heavy footsteps.

"In the living room," Percy said.

All eyes turned to the woman as she entered, followed by Franklin and Vasquez.

"Someone left the gate open," Lori swept back wet strands of hair from her face. "Bella and several other horses got out of the corrals. I don't see them anywhere."

Franklin stepped forward, water dripping from his cowboy hat. "To make matters worse, the sky just opened up and it's raining like there's no tomorrow."

"Did you try honking the truck horn," Percy asked. "They usually come back to the sound. It means feeding time."

Hannah shook her head, thinking of all the places Bella might have gone. "To most of the horses, but not Bella. She might head back into the hills again. That wolf pack had been on the other side of the fence. They could have crossed onto Brighter Days." Hannah stepped out of Taz's arms. "Is Frisco still in his stall?"

"Yes, ma'am," Franklin said. "I just cleaned the stall and put him in with fresh straw."

"What other horses are still close?" she asked.

"Little Joe was hanging around the back of the barn. He didn't leave with the others," Vasquez said.

"Good." Hannah shot a glance at her father, still too shocked by the revelation for the reality to sink in. "We will talk later. Right now, I have a horse to catch, before the wolves get her." When she spun away, Taz, Percy, Gavin, Lori, Vasquez and Franklin blocked her path.

Young pushed into the room, covered in mud. "Thanks for leaving me in the barn. Did you tell her?"

Franklin nodded. "We did. And she thinks she's going out to find them."

"The hell she is," Gavin said.

Taz crossed his arms over his chest. "You're not going,"

She lifted her chin. "I'm going after Bella."

"You'll let us take care of her," Gavin insisted.

"I can't stand around the house while that poor horse is out there. Those wolves were hungry. Bella's a loner. She'll be an easy target."

"You're not going," Taz repeated. "Nash could be out there. He could have been the one to release the horses to lure you away into the open."

"The man is too lazy to get out in the cold rain," Hannah argued. When she attempted to step around Taz, he moved in front of her.

The others in the room tightened up their blockade.

Hannah knew she wouldn't get past all of them. "Fine. I won't go alone. Besides, we'll need everyone to look for the horses and bring them back. Bella could be almost anywhere." She turned to Taz. "You can come with me and be my bodyguard. I won't argue. But I have to be out there, too. We have to find Bella. She's been through so much already."

Hannah held Taz's gaze until he let out a long, slow breath. She wasn't sure he'd cave. The man had his own ideas about how to protect her. But Hannah could be just as stubborn as anyone, woman or man.

"You'll stay with me? No wandering off?"

She crossed a finger over her heart. "Promise."

Taz inhaled and let go of the breath slowly. "Okay, on one condition."

"What condition?" she asked.

"You wear a Kevlar vest."

Her brow furrowed. "A what?"

"A bullet-proof vest."

She smiled. "Deal."

"Then let's go find a horse."

Hannah and Taz turned to face a lineup of Percy, Gavin, Franklin, Vasquez, Young and Lori.

Hannah laughed. "What? I have to convince all of you, too?"

Percy held his cowboy hat in his hand. "I lost your mother three years ago. I don't want to lose you, too. You're my family."

Gavin tapped his thigh. "No telling where I'd be now if you hadn't roped me into this gig. Probably dead in a gutter somewhere."

Hannah's eyes teared. "No way. You're invincible," she said, her voice catching.

Franklin nodded toward Vasquez and Young. "We need our best therapist. You kick our asses into shape and won't let us be slackers."

"We need you." Lori hugged her. "So don't go getting yourself killed, dammit."

Hannah swallowed hard on the lump in her throat. "I'm not going to get myself killed. I'm going to keep an ornery horse, that's still recovering from being practically starved to death, from being eaten by wolves."

"We're going with you," her clients all said as one.

"The ground is muddy out there and it's dangerous. We only had two horses in their stalls. I'm taking one of them and Taz will ride the other. How will the rest of you get out there?"

"We'll take the truck as far as we can go," Franklin said.

Percy nodded toward Hannah. "I'll take them out along the roads I know won't be slippery yet."

"I can handle a four-wheeler," Lori said.

Hannah hesitated, and then nodded. "You and Gavin can take the ATVs." She clapped her hands together. "Let's go. The longer we wait, the worse the conditions."

She glanced at the senator. "Will you be here

when I return?"

He shook his head. "After I make a stop at the sheriff's office to give him a statement, I need to get my wife back to Bozeman."

When Hannah's gaze met Holloway's.

He gave her a brief nod. "I guess that makes us step-siblings." He raised his hand. "I won't be here when you get back. I'm going with my mother to get her...settled. But I'll return in a week. We have a lot to talk about."

"Agreed." But for now, she had a more pressing concern. Without wasting anymore time, she ran for the back door, slipped into her mud boots and raincoat and hurried across the yard. She was in the barn, saddling Frisco, when Taz and the others caught up.

Taz had returned to his room for boots, a jacket, a rifle and the Kevlar vest. He helped Hannah into the vest.

"Dang, it's heavy," she said, shrugging her shoulders to adjust to the added weight."

"The better to stop bullets." He kissed her and then made quick work of saddling Little Joe, he slipped the rifle into the scabbard, bridled the horse and followed Hannah out of the barn.

Percy had honked the truck horn several times while they'd been in the barn. Half a dozen horses and several cows came running across the pasture through the torrential rain.

Gavin caught Hannah's arm. "Wait for Lori and I to get the four-wheelers going."

Hannah shook off his hand. "I cant. You'll

be headed in a different direction anyway. Please…be careful. If Troy is out there, he might mistake Lori for me."

"Like you said, I seriously doubt Nash will be out in this mess. But, Hannah—"

Gavin's words held her as she placed her foot in the stirrup. "Yes, Gavin?"

"Don't do anything stupid." Gavin glanced up at Taz who'd already mounted his horse and plunked his cowboy hat onto his head. "If something happens to her…"

"I'll take care of her," he said, rain dripping from the brim of his hat and running off the shoulders of his jacket.

Hannah's heart swelled. With Taz at her back, she was invincible.

Chapter 15

Taz questioned his decision to allow Hannah to leave the house, especially when Troy Nash was unaccounted for. His Ranger training taught him never to take a new recruit on a dangerous mission. Yet, here he was, taking Hannah out in the cold rain to find a horse.

But he knew Hannah wouldn't stay at the house when a sick horse was in trouble. Her caring nature was one of things he loved about the therapist.

She didn't hold back on her emotions. And she gave one hundred percent in everything she did. A little rain, a pack of wolves and a psycho assassin wouldn't stop her.

At least, Taz hoped Troy wasn't successful in his attempt to hurt Hannah.

Taz rode alongside her, scanning the tree line, brush and hills all around them. The rain limited his field of vision, blurring what he could see and making it hard for him to find the missing horse.

The truck followed at a distance, loaded with Hannah's clients, eager to help her in any way. They turned toward the south pasture, Gavin and Lori rode west, while Hannah and Taz headed north where they'd originally found Bella.

Once they slipped into the hills, Taz lost

sight of the others, but he stayed right with Hannah, hovering so close his leg bumped hers several times.

Rain ran off Hannah's cowboy hat onto her hands holding the reins. She hunkered into her jacket, her blue jean-clad thighs soaked through. She didn't complain about the cold, nor did she turn back. And she wouldn't, until she brought Bella with her.

In a valley with steep hills flanking either side, Hannah led the way along the banks of a creek, swelled with runoff from the rain.

Taz got more than a chill of rain sliding down his spine. Call it intuition, a premonition or a hunch, a niggling feeling made the hair on the back of his neck bristle. Someone was following them and getting closer.

Looking over his shoulder, Taz swore he saw a figure duck behind a tree. He rested his hand on the rifle in the scabbard. When they rounded the bend in the narrow valley, he spied an outcropping of rocks.

As he neared it, he reached across and touched her arm. Then he slipped off Little Joe and handed his reins to Hannah. "Lead the horses deeper into this pile of boulders and hunker down low."

Her brows furrowed and she shot a glance toward Taz, questioning him without saying a word.

He slipped his hand beneath his jacket, pulled out his nine-millimeter pistol and placed it in her hands. "Use this, if you have to." He smiled and winked. "Just don't shoot me. I'll be back in a few minutes."

He dragged the rifle from the scabbard and waited for her to hide in the boulders. When he couldn't see her anymore, he hugged the darkest edges of the giant rocks and worked his way backward along the trail without showing himself to whoever might be following.

He'd gone several hundred yards when he noticed a rivulet of water rushing toward the stream, like so many others in the downpour. Only this once wasn't muddy or clear. The water was the deep, dark shade of blood.

Gripping his rifle at the ready, he inched his way through a stand of trees and around a clump of brush where he found a man lying facedown, blood running from beneath him into a stream heading toward the creek.

At once taking up a defensive position, Taz put his back to the inert form and stared into the rain and shadows. He placed his hand on the body. It was still warm. Intent on searching for a pulse, Taz shoved the man onto his back. That's when he realized he wouldn't find a pulse.

The man's throat had been slashed all the way across, severing the jugular. No amount of CPR would help him now. He was dead, though his body was still warm.

Taz recognized the man as Troy Nash from the day before when he'd fired at the wolves, nearly hitting Hannah.

Damn. Whoever had killed him was still out there and very close by.

That Troy was dead created a huge and gaping hole in their search for who was terrorizing Hannah.

And Taz had left her alone. He leaped to his feet and emerged from behind the brush, scanning the area for movement.

His pulse slamming through his veins, Taz raced back the way he'd come, not giving a damn whether he was seen. Fear filled his gut. Hannah was in danger. He picked up the pace and would have run all the way back to her, but a man stepped out in front of him holding an AR15 semi-automatic rifle to his shoulder.

Taz slid, stumbled and jerked to a halt, memories spinning through his head, images flashing like a kaleidoscope of colors and faces. One face materialized from the darkness of an Afghan building, his arm swinging out to toss a grenade.

"You!" Taz choked on the betrayal. "You threw the grenade that killed my team."

"Took you long enough to remember." Staff Sergeant Jeff Hix, who'd been a trusted member of their platoon of Army Rangers, pointed a weapon at Taz's chest. All the memories that had been scrambled when the grenade exploded and the wall crashed down on Taz now came flooding back into his head. The one image he had fought the most to remember was that of the man who'd been in that room when his world had come completely apart.

"You son of a bitch!" Taz started to raise his rifle.

"I wouldn't do that if I were you," Hix said. "Toss it, or I'll shoot you. And then what will become of your pretty little cowgirl?"

Taz stood stiff, his instinct to crash into the coward and rip him apart tempered by reality. He couldn't let the bastard get to Hannah. He bent to lay the rifle on the ground and then straightened. "Why did you come all the way out here? Why are you doing this?"

"I don't plan on going to jail. I had it all figured out. Blow up the room where I'd made some pretty lucrative deals, destroying any chance of them tying me to the weapons trading. Only, you got there faster than I expected. When you opened that door and saw my face, I had no choice."

"You killed McC, Guthrie and K-man," Taz said through gritted teeth, anger boiling in his veins. "They trusted you."

Hix shrugged. "Collateral damage. You were the one who should have died. But, I swear to God, you're like a damned cat with nine lives. No matter how many times I tried, you just wouldn't die."

Taz's fists clenched. "You were the one who tried to run me over twice in DC?"

"Who knew a man who'd had to relearn how to walk and talk could move so damned fast?"

"And the drive-by shooting wasn't just a

random thug?"

"What can I say?" His lips curled into a snarl. "It's hard to aim straight when you're driving."

"You never were that good a shot, Hix."

The man's eyes narrowed. "I didn't have to be. I just had to be a good negotiator. I made a killing selling those weapons. When my deployment was over last month, I came back to the States to make sure the one loose thread was snipped."

Taz teeth ground together. "Me."

"But this is where it ends. No more mistakes. This is your ninth life, and it's about to end."

"You aren't going to get away with it." He couldn't. Taz had to live to save Hannah from this psychopath.

"Actually, I will." With his weapon carefully aimed at Taz's chest, Hix glanced at his watch. "In exactly one minute, an earthen dam upstream will explode. Thousands of gallons of lake water will flood this little valley, sending your dead body so far downstream it will be weeks before they find you. By then, I'll be sipping Mai Tais in a tropical paradise far from this godforsaken country. Nobody will tag me as a traitor, a man who sold American weapons to the enemy. I'll take my money and disappear."

"Why didn't you just do that? Why follow me all the way to Montana and risk being caught?"

Hix's chest puffed out. "I received a purple heart and a bronze star for my service in that shithole. My parents and my old unit think I'm a hero. That's all they should know."

As far as Taz was concerned, the man had to die. "You're a fool, a traitor and a murderer. You deserve to rot in hell."

"Yeah, maybe so, but you're the one who will have that pleasure." Hix tipped his head and glanced through the scope. "Now, die."

Taz hadn't cheated death so many times only to be shot and killed by a goddamn traitor. And if he didn't do something quickly, Hannah would die with him. With only one chance to save his ass and get to Hannah before that dam exploded, Taz ducked and threw himself into a somersault. He barreled into Hix's legs, knocking the man off his feet.

The AR15 flew into the air and clattered against the rocks as it hit the ground.

Hix landed on his back, his head bouncing off a boulder.

Taz rolled to his feet and lunged for the fallen AR15, snatching it from the ground. He pointed it at Hix's chest, his breaths coming in ragged gasps. He only had seconds before Hix's charge exploded. Still he hesitated.

The man lay on the ground, staring up at the sky, huge raindrops splashing in his face. He didn't blink, didn't try to get up. Hix lay as still as death.

Taz nudged him with his boot. Finally, he squatted down on his haunches and felt for a pulse. "I'll be damned," Taz muttered.

The man who'd tried so many times to kill

him was dead, having smashed his head on a rock.

With no time to spare, Taz leaped to his feet and raced toward Hannah.

Hannah shivered in the rain, waiting for Taz to return. After several minutes, the lack of movement made her so cold she couldn't stand still any longer. She left the horses and eased through the boulder-strewn maze. When she could see the creek, she carefully poked her head around the corner of an outcropping, searching for Taz, praying Troy wasn't out there looking to gun him down.

The usually lazy creek had swelled to twice its size, the water from upstream tumbling over the rocks, creating brown, frothy rapids.

Hannah's pulse quickened. Flash floods were a real threat in the mountains. Taz might not be aware of the signs.

On the other side of the rushing brook was a patch of grass and a steep rise, leading out of the rugged valley. At the edge of the grassy patch was a dark blotch. It moved. A head rose above the blotch.

Hannah blinked the water from her eyes and squinted through the torrents of rain. The head shook, a dark, wet mane slapping against a thick neck.

Bella.

Glancing left and then right, Hannah didn't see anyone coming or going. She'd come to find Bella. The horse was across the creek. In order to get to her, she had to cross.

But she couldn't do it with the Kevlar vest on. If she fell into the creek, she'd drown before she could unclip all of the buckles.

Making the decision, she shed the vest, pushing aside the twinge of guilt. Taz had placed the vest on her to keep her safe.

Knowing she was too light to cross the creek on her own, she ran back to the horses, mounted Frisco, looped Little Joe's reins over her saddle horn and trotted out of the safety of the boulders, urging Frisco into the roiling, churning water.

He danced sideways, at first refusing to take the plunge.

Little Joe, the calm, steady influence waded in first.

Frisco, seeing the other horse getting ahead of him, followed, moving fast enough to take the lead. Several times the horses slipped on the rocks, but remained upright in the increasing force of the rain-swollen creek.

Hannah held on to the saddle horn and Little Joe's reins, her gaze on Bella, praying the mare wouldn't take off running as soon as she noticed the other two horses heading her way.

Once they arrived safely on the other side of the creek, Hannah dismounted and dropped their reins. Each horse had been trained to remain close when their reins dangled to the ground.

She removed the coiled lead rope looped around the saddle horn and turned toward the escaped mare. Moving slowly, Hannah crept toward Bella, talking in low, steady tones. "Hey, pretty girl. Come to Hannah. I just want to help you."

Bella raised her head, her ears perking up and her nostrils flaring. Rain had drenched her shaggy coat, exposing the pathetic outline of her ribs.

"Oh, Bella." Hannah cast another glance around, checking upstream and down. Still, she didn't see anyone coming. When she was within two feet of the mare, she slowly raised her hand, palm up, pretending to have a treat.

While Bella snuffled her lips across Hannah's open palm, Hannah snagged the mare's halter and snapped the lead onto the metal ring. As the metal clip locked in place, a loud boom sounded, shaking the earth beneath her feet.

Bella reared, screaming in fright.

The lead ripped through Hannah's hand, burning her palm. She grabbed with her other hand and held on, the pain searing up her arm. But she couldn't let go. If she did, she'd never catch the mare again.

Frisco and Little Joe raced past Hannah, climbing up the steep hill, slipping and sliding, churning the loose, saturated soil.

Bella strained against the lead, dragging Hannah as she followed the other two horses. As soon as Bella started up the hill, her hooves slipped in the mud and she fell to her knees.

Hannah staggered to her feet.

A rumbling sound grew in intensity, like a runaway train barreling down a mountainside.

The swollen creek spread out, covering the grassy knoll.

Hannah narrowed her eyes, peering through the rain, looking upstream in the direction of the strengthening roar. What appeared to be a tidal wave rushed toward her, carrying with it trees, rocks and anything else that dared be in its path.

Her heart stopped, and she froze for a split second. Then she was pulling, tugging and half-dragging the terrified mare up the slippery slope, her shoulders aching with the strain.

Bella fought to get her feet beneath her, her strength so near to giving out. Then, just when Hannah thought they had no hope, Bella's hooves found purchase and she clambered up the hillside.

Hannah held on as best she could, but rain and blood from her raw hands made gripping the lead impossible. Before she reached the top, the rope slid free of her grip. Hannah fell backward, tumbling downward toward the roiling floodwaters. She flattened her body against the muddy slope and dug her fingers and her boot tips into the ground, but nothing slowed her descent.

When she slipped into the water, it surged over her head, dragging her under. She kicked and fought her way to the surface only to be rolled and sucked under again. Her lungs burning and her sense of up and down scrambled, Hannah had all but given up hope when she slammed into a tree branch. Waves splashed in her face as she clung to the branch and gasped for air. She worked her way higher up the tree, praying it wouldn't fall victim to the force of hundreds of thousands of gallons of water rushing down the mountain.

When she'd gone as far as she had strength to, she wedged herself into a fork and waited out the flood, hoping beyond hope Taz had made it out alive.

Chapter 16

Taz heard the explosion and the subsequent roar of a lake full of water rushing through the narrow valley. Running as fast as his feet could carry him, he reached the stand of boulders as the creek water began to swell.

Hannah and the horses weren't there. Taz's heart sank. Out of time, he ran up the side of a hill, aiming for several dark holes that appeared to be caves. With rain still pelting him and the ground, Taz's feet slipped on the gravel rise. For every two steps he slid backward one. A glance over his shoulder toward the source of the floodwaters made his blood chill.

A wall of ugly, churning water rushed toward him, gobbling up everything in its path.

This was it. Either he lived or died.

With a final burst of effort and balance, he clawed his way up the gravel slope and collapsed on the floor of what turned out to be a shallow cave.

Taking only a moment to catch his breath, Taz staggered to his feet and turned to watch the valley floor on which he'd walked seconds before disappear beneath the torrent. He scanned the ridges on either side of the river, desperately searching for Hannah. Then he saw them. Three horses, crowded onto a small hilltop surrounded by water. His heart plummeted when he didn't see Hannah anywhere nearby.

"Oh, darlin'," he moaned. "I shouldn't have left you. I shouldn't have gone." Once again, he'd failed the people he cared most about.

Throat tight and chest heaving, Taz dropped to his knees and buried his head in his hands. What good was his life to live if he continued to fail the people who mattered?

Moments passed. The thunderous roar of the flash flood subsided as the swell of water swept farther downstream.

Taz almost wished he'd been swept away with the floodwaters. But Hannah would have wanted him to save the horses and get them safely back to the barn. He couldn't give up now. Frisco, Little Joe and Bella needed him.

As the water returned to the original level of the rain-swollen creek, Taz slid down the hillside, dodging the debris left behind by the receding waters.

He crossed the stream, almost getting swept away by the rushing waters. When he reached the other side, he clicked his tongue and called out, "Frisco, Little Joe, Bella,"

All three horses turned toward him.

Taz whistled.

Frisco was first to start down the muddy slope.

Bella hesitated.

Little Joe nipped her lightly on the flank.

The emaciated mare danced sideways and

then surprised Taz by following Frisco to the bottom. Little Joe slid down the mud and trotted up to Taz, nuzzling his jacket, searching for a treat.

Taz took some comfort in saving Hannah's horses.

The rain lightened and eventually stopped as Taz gathered Frisco and Little Joe's reins. When he reached for Bella's lead, he realized the horse shouldn't have had a lead unless Hannah had found her and snapped it on her bridle. Hope swelled.

Could she have made it to higher ground before the floodwaters swept through the valley?

He turned and yelled as loud as he could. "Hannah!" Taz stood still and listened.

Again, he yelled, "Hannah!"

His voice echoed off the cliff sides.

For a moment he thought all he heard was the echo. Then another sound made his heart flutter.

"Hannah?" he said. With the reins and Bella's lead in hand, he ran downstream. "Hannah!" He couldn't hear over the sound of the horses' hooves so he stopped to listen.

"Taz?"

His heart beating so fast it made him dizzy, Taz searched all around but couldn't find Hannah. Yet, he heard her voice. "Hannah, please, tell me where you are? Please," he said, his voice choking on the knot rising in his throat.

"Sweet Jesus," she cried softly. "Look up."

When he did, he laughed until he felt tears slipping down his cheeks. "Hannah, baby, how in hell did you get way up in that tree?"

"Funny you should ask." She chuckled. "Get me down from here, and I'll tell you. I don't know how much longer I can hold on."

He studied the tree. Only a few lower branches remained. He tied the horses together and started up the tree, pulling himself up from one limb to the next.

"What are you doing?"

"Coming to rescue the damsel in distress," he said, swinging from one limb to another. A few more branches and he'd be on her level.

"Taz, what if you get dizzy?" she asked.

"I already am. Crazy, dizzy for you."

She laughed, the sound more of a sob. "I was worried about you," she said softly.

"Oh, babe, I thought I'd lost you. You have no idea how happy I was to hear your voice. Even coming from the heavens." He pulled himself up to the limb beside her and braced himself against the trunk. "Come here."

"I don't know if I can." She unwound one arm from the branch and reached out.

Taz clasped her hand.

When she released the branch all together, she slipped sideways and would have fallen out of the tree, if Taz hadn't been holding on.

He yanked her into his arms and held her there, his legs wrapped around the branch he sat on. "Shh. You're okay, now."

"I was so afraid," she whispered against his neck. "I thought you were dead."

"Not even a flood can finish me off. I was more worried about you." He hugged, not wanting to let go, ever again.

"Taz?"

"Yeah, babe?"

"I can't breathe."

He loosened his hold, just enough to make her comfortable, but not enough to drop her.

"How are we getting down from here?" she asked.

"I don't know. We might need another miracle."

The sound of rotor blades filled the air a moment before a sleek black helicopter rose up over a ridge to hover over the valley.

Taz had never seen a more welcome sight. He waved an arm over his head, praying he'd be seen in the branches of the tree.

The chopper hovered for several seconds, while Taz held his breath, wondering if the pilot had seen them trapped in the tree.

Then the side door opened on the aircraft and a man was lowered on a cable. Another man stood near the open door.

Hank Patterson. He waved at Taz and waited while the man on the cable wrapped a harness around Hannah and then held her steady as they were reeled up into the helicopter.

The cable descended again and Taz wrapped the harness around himself. When they pulled him up into the helicopter, he spoke to Patterson. "Make them wait."

Patterson said something into his headset and gave Taz a thumbs-up.

Hannah lay on a stretcher on the floor. Taz bent over her. "Hey, are you going to be okay?"

She nodded.

He pressed a kiss to her forehead. "I'll see you later.

Then Taz turned to Patterson. "You have to lower me to the valley floor."

"Why?"

He pointed out the open door to the horses on the ground below. "I have to get them back to the barn."

Patterson nodded and motioned to the man operating the controls.

Taz stepped out on the skid, dangled beside the door and then sank to the floor of the valley, his heart full, and a smile spreading across his face. Then he mounted Little Joe, climbed out of the ravaged valley and led Bella and Frisco back toward the barn.

He couldn't wait to get back to Hannah and hold her in his arms. She had a helluva story to tell him. But, he had one of his own. Thankfully, they'd both lived to tell them.

Chapter 17

Hannah sat on the edge of the couch in the Brighter Days ranch house, looking around a room full of the people she loved. Her heart was so full, she thought it might explode.

The senator had come for a visit as promised. Her stepbrother, Martin was there. Franklin, Vasquez, Young and Lori sat nearby, talking about the puppies, celebrating the fact Sydney had taken Lucky back into the fold and now fed him along with the rest of his siblings.

Gavin and Percy discussed the new tractor they'd ordered to replace the one that had been destroyed.

The only person missing from the group was Taz. Since the deaths of Troy Nash and Jeff Hix, Hannah wasn't being targeted by anyone. Her world was once again safe. She had no need for a bodyguard. But she really missed having him around all the time.

A week had passed since the explosion and her trip via helicopter to the hospital in Bozeman. Released the same afternoon, she'd been flown to the ranch in the same helicopter belonging to Hank Patterson's Brotherhood Protectors organization.

Taz had been there, after bringing the horses back to the barn and taken care of them. He'd stayed most of the week to make sure she was all right and to answer questions for the sheriff.

Taz had left the day before and she hadn't seen nor heard from him since. Before he'd gone, though, he'd promised to take her on a date, and tonight was the night.

In another nice surprise, Hannah's father had picked that morning to arrive for the visit he'd promised. Hannah was glad for the time to get to know him, and she'd spent the day showing him the ranch, introducing him to every veteran and rescue animal. She wanted him to know what her life was like, and she wanted him to be proud of what she did.

As she sat beside him on the couch, she couldn't remember a time she'd been happier since her mother's death. "I'm glad you could come to see me, Senator Buchanan."

"Please, senator is so formal. I know I haven't been much of a father to you, but I'd love it if you called me James."

She nodded, liking the sound of the compromise. "James."

"I realize my mistake in waiting so long. I knew my wife was ill, but I didn't realize just how ill she was. I hope you will one day forgive me."

Hannah reached out and touched his hand. "Already have. But, tell me, what about Brighter Days Ranch? Now that I know who you are, you don't have to own a ranch to keep me here. Do you want to continue our work here?"

The room grew silent, and all gazes turned

toward the senator.

He smiled and nodded. "I've heard so many good things about the ranch, I would never shut it down. The veterans need this place as much as the horses they help rescue. I'm impressed by all you've done to get this operation going."

Hannah's heart swelled. "I'm glad you feel that way. This ranch has always been my home. Here, I feel closer to my mother than anywhere else. She was a good woman and the best mother I could have asked for."

The senator stared down at his hands. "I wish she would have let me know about you. I feel like I missed so much." He looked up, capturing her gaze. "I don't even know you."

Glad to hear that he regretted missing out on her life, Hannah smiled. "We have the rest of our lives to get to know each other. I could come visit you in Bozeman."

"And I'd love to come spend time with the veterans and horses. I could even help out when I'm here."

She pushed to her feet. "I'll take you up on that, especially when we cut our next field of hay."

"I'm game." The senator rose to stand beside her. "But go easy on me, I'm an old man."

She snorted. Her father was older, but he must have had a really good exercise program, because he was fit and healthy. "I hate to leave you now, but I have somewhere I need to be."

"Don't let me keep you, Hannah. Like you

said, we have the rest of our lives to get to know each other."

She started to walk away, changed her mind, turned to her father and flung her arms around him, giving him a big hug.

He hugged her back with equal fervor.

Hannah leaned away and grinned. "I've always wanted to hug my father. Now I have. And it felt good. I'll see you soon?"

He nodded, his eyes shiny with moisture. "You bet."

Hannah hurried toward the front door, the skirt of her powder-blue dress whirling around her calves, her new, low-heel strappy sandals making her feel sexy and pretty, giving her a lift in her steps.

When she opened the front door, Taz stood there with his hand raised, ready to knock.

"Well, aren't you lovely?" he said. "Ready?"

God, he was so handsome. And he was there for her. Hannah had never felt so very lucky. "I've been ready for over a week. Where are we going on our first date?"

"I have a special surprise for you." He drew her out onto the porch and wrapped his arms around her waist.

"Really," she said, raising her face to his for the kiss.

He didn't disappoint, brushing his lips across hers ever so lightly before crashing down and claiming her mouth in a hungry, crazy, soul-defining connection.

When he finally let her come up for air, he leaned back. "Did you pack a bag for a weekend trip, like I asked?"

She nodded. "I did."

"Good, because you can make one of two choices. The first is we fly to Seattle for the weekend. I have a buddy who has a condo with an incredible view overlooking the ocean. Hank's friend will fly us there in just a few short hours in his turbo prop airplane."

She smiled, impressed. "Sounds lovely. What's my other choice?"

"Dinner at the Blue Moose Tavern. And, if you want, we can spend a weekend in the mountains, alone in a cabin next to a lake. We can fish, watch the sunrise and sunset or..." his voice lowered to a deep, sexy tone, "We can just make love until the weekend's over."

"And what choice did you think I would make?"

Taz grinned. "Mountain cabin and skip the tavern."

"Ranger boy, what are you waiting for? We have an entire weekend to get started." Hannah grabbed the bag by the door in one hand and Taz's arm in the other and led him down the stairs.

He pulled her to a stop as they reached the ground. "And when this weekend is over, what then? Now that you don't need a bodyguard anymore, I won't see you every day."

She stared up at him. "Sweet Jesus, Taz, you

don't have to be my bodyguard to see me every day. And now that you have your memory back, you don't need me as a therapist." Hannah cupped his cheek. "But I like having you around. If this dating thing works out, which I have a feeling it will, we might be seeing a lot more of each other."

He laughed and pulled her into his arms again. "That's music to this Ranger's ears."

She brushed his lips with a light kiss, hooked her arm through his elbow and led him to his truck. Once inside the cab, she leaned across the console and kissed the man. "Yeah, I don't think I'll get tired of this anytime soon. I hope you don't."

"Not a chance, sweetheart. Not a chance." He cupped her cheeks in his hands and stared into her eyes. "You're everything I could have wished for in a woman, and so much more."

About the Author

ELLE JAMES also writing as MYLA JACKSON is a *New York Times* and *USA Today* Bestselling author of books including cowboys, intrigues and paranormal adventures that keep her readers on the edges of their seats. With over eighty works in a variety of sub-genres and lengths she has published with Harlequin, Samhain, Ellora's Cave, Kensington, Cleis Press, and Avon. When she's not at her computer, she's traveling, snow skiing, boating, or riding her ATV, dreaming up new stories.

Learn more about Elle James at
www.ellejames.com

Or visit her alter ego Myla Jackson at
www.mylajackson.com

TAKE NO PRISONERS
TUCK & DELANEY
BOOK 1

SEAL's Honor

New York Times & USA Today Bestselling Author

ELLE JAMES

SEAL's Honor

Take No Prisoners Series

Book #1

Elle James

New York Times Bestselling Author

Chapter 1

REED TUCKER, Tuck to his buddies, tugged at the tie on his U.S. Navy service dress blue uniform, and his gut knotted as he entered the rehabilitation center of the National Naval Medical Center in Bethesda, Maryland.

He'd never run from anything, not a machine gun pinning his unit to a position, a fight where he was outnumbered, or an argument he truly believed in. But the sights, smells, and sounds inside the walls of the rehabilitation center made him want to get the hell out of the facility faster than a cat with its tail on fire.

But he couldn't leave. Not yet. This was graduation day for Reaper, aka Cory Nipton, his best friend and former teammate on SEAL Team 10. Reaper was being released from the rehabilitation center after enduring something even tougher than BUD/s training, the twenty-four-week Basic Underwater Demolition/SEAL training designed to weed out the true SEALs from the wannabes.

But Reaper's release from rehab wasn't the only event that brought Tuck there that day. He was going to a wedding. His heart twisted, his palms grew clammy, and he clutched the ring box in his left hand as regret warred with guilt, creating a vile taste in his mouth.

Reaper was marrying Delaney, the only

1

woman Tuck had ever trusted with his heart. The only woman who'd forced him to get over his past and dare to dream of a future. She was the woman he could see himself spending the rest of his life with. And today she was promising to love, honor, and cherish his best friend—a better man than Tuck by far. A hero who'd lost his right arm because Tuck hadn't given him sufficient cover. Cory deserved all the happiness he could get after being medically discharged out of the only family he'd ever known. The Navy SEALs.

His hand on the door to the room where the wedding was to take place, Tuck squared his shoulders and stepped into his future.

Two months earlier

Tuck glanced to his left and right. The members of Strike Force Dragon sat or stood, tense, holding onto whatever they could as the MH-60M Black Hawk dipped into the valley between two hilltops, less than a click away from the dark, quiet village. The only thing different about this mission was that, since the one before, he'd slept with the Pilot in Command of the helicopter.

Most men knew her as Razor, the call sign they used for the only female pilot flying infiltration and extraction missions for the 160th Special Operations Aviation Regiment (SOAR), Army Captain Delaney O'Connell.

Through his NVGs he picked up the bright green signature of a lookout on top of one of the buildings.

Within seconds, shots were fired at them, tracer rounds flaring in the dark. The helicopter remained just out of range of the man's rifle shots, but it wouldn't be long before a Taliban machine gunner with long-range capability was alerted with the potential of lobbing rocket-propelled grenades their way.

Wasting no time, the helicopter sank to a level just above the drop zone (DZ). While it hovered the men fast-roped down.

As soon as his boots hit the ground, Tuck brought up his M4A1 in the ready position and ran toward the sniper on the rooftop, zigzagging to avoid being locked in the enemy crosshairs.

Reaper, Big Bird, Gator, Fish, and Dustman spread out to the sides and followed.

When they were in range, Reaper took a knee and employed his uncanny ability as a sharpshooter to knock off the sentry on the rooftop.

The team continued forward into the walled town, going from building to building, until they reached the one they were after. In the center of the compound, high walls surrounded one particular brick and mud structure.

Big Bird bent and cupped his hands.

Tuck planted his boot in the man's massive paws and, with Big Bird's help, launched himself to the top of the wall, dropping down on the other side in a crouch. Weapon pointing at the building, finger on the trigger, Tuck scanned the courtyard for potential threat. People moved past windows inside. So far, no one had stepped outside to check out the disturbance. Only a matter of time. "Clear," he said into his headset.

As Dustman topped the wall, a man emerged from the side of the structure and fired on them.

Without hesitation, Tuck fired off a silent round, downing the man with one bullet.

Dustman dropped to the ground beside him and gave him a thumbs up, taking the position by the wall so Tuck could move to the corner where the dead man lay.

As they'd discussed in the operations briefing, they only had three minutes to get into the compound, retrieve their target, and get out. Kill anyone in the way, but bring out the target alive.

Once four of the six-man team were inside the wall, they breached the doorway and entered, moving from room to room. If someone or something moved, they had only a millisecond to decide whether or not to shoot.

Tuck opened the first room. Inside, small green heat signatures glowed in his NVGs. Children sleeping on mats on the floor. He eased shut the door, jamming a wedge in the gap to keep them from getting out too soon.

He moved on to the next room. When he opened the door, a woman rose from a pallet, wearing a long black burka. When she lifted her hand like she held a gun, Tuck fired, taking her down before she could pull the trigger.

As he continued in the lead position down

the narrow hallway, Tuck's adrenaline hammered blood through his veins and honed his senses. His wits in hyper-alert status, his finger rested a hair's breadth away from again pulling the trigger. This was the life he was made for. Defending his country, seeking out his enemies and destroying them with a swift, deadly strike. His job was risky, dangerous, and deadly.

A man emerged from a room down the hall.

Tuck's nerves spiked. He had only a fraction of a second to identify him.

Not his target.

He pulled the trigger and nailed him with another silent round. The man slumped to the floor, his cry for help nothing more than a startled gasp.

The door he'd emerged from flew open and men bearing guns poured out.

Tuck spoke quietly into his headset. "Get down." He didn't bother to look back. His team would follow his orders without hesitation. He dropped with them, his M4A1 in front of him, and fired at the kneecaps of the men filling the hallway.

One by one, they went down, discharging their weapons, the bullets going wide and high.

In Pashto, the language spoken by most of the population of Afghanistan and Pakistan, Tuck told them to lay down their weapons.

When one of the injured enemies sat up and took aim, Tuck fired another round, putting him out of the game.

The injured enemy soldiers threw down their guns.

"Gator, clean up out here," Tuck whispered into his mic. "Reaper and Big Bird, you're with me."

In the lead, Tuck stepped around the fallen Taliban and entered the room in a low crouch, ducking to the right. Nothing moved. Another door led into yet another unknown space. Tuck dove into the room and rolled to the side, weapon up.

As he entered, a man with an AK47 fired off a burst of rounds that whizzed past Tuck's ears, missing him, but not by much. The man shouted for Tuck to drop his weapon.

Tuck fired at the shooter's chest. He fell to the ground, revealing the man he'd been protecting. Their target, the Taliban leader they'd been briefed on. He stood straight, a pistol aimed at Tuck.

Though he wanted to pull the trigger, Tuck couldn't shoot. His mission was to bring him out alive.

His hesitation cost him. A round, fired pointblank, hit him in the chest and flung him backward to land on his ass. If not for the armor plate protecting him, he'd be a dead man. He lay still for a moment, struggling to regulate his breathing.

Reaper used the stun gun, firing off a round that hit dead on and had the man flat on his back and twitching in seconds. "You okay?" He extended his hand to help Tuck to his feet.

"Yeah." Tuck motioned to Big Bird. "Take him."

The biggest, strongest man of the team, Big Bird lifted their target and flung him over his shoulder.

Still fighting to catch his breath, Tuck led the way back to the fence. Once outside the building, he scanned his surroundings and then checked back up at the top of the roof. No signs of enemy snipers. But that didn't mean they were in the clear. They still had to navigate their way out of town and get back to the helicopter.

Leading the way, with Gator and Fish guarding the rear, Tuck hurried back along the narrow street to the outer walls of the village where the helicopter hovered nearby, waiting for their signal.

Tuck blinked the flashlight outfitted with a red lens at the hovering aircraft and it moved in, setting down for the briefest of moments, enough to get the six-man team inside. He reached over the back of the seat to the pilot and shouted, "Go!"

The Black Hawk lurched into the air, rising up and moving forward at the same time, hurrying to gain as much altitude as possible as they disappeared into the night sky, out of enemy sight and weapons range.

Not until they were well out of reach did Tuck release the breath he'd been holding and take stock of his team and their prisoner. All of them made it out alive and intact. That's the way he liked it. He'd been the only one who would have sustained injury if he hadn't been equipped with armor plating.

The co-pilot handed Tuck an aviation headset and he slipped it on.

"Nine minutes, twenty-five seconds." Gunnery Sergeant Sullivan's raspy voice sounded in Tuck's ear. "Better, but still not fast enough."

This had been a training mission; one they'd repeated five times in the past two weeks. Someone wanted them to get it right. The team was improving, but still needed to be quieter, faster, and more aware when the mission was real. The people they'd shot tonight had only been tagged with lasers. If this mission went live, the ammunition used against them would be live rounds.

Leaning back, Tuck held up nine fingers for his team to see and understand the repercussions of wearing out their welcome in a Taliban-held village.

The men nodded. Noise from the rotors precluded talking inside the chopper. When they got back to the base at Little Creek, Virginia, they'd debrief before being dismissed for the night and hitting the club.

They'd played the same scenario five times, improving with each iteration. All six members of the team were highly skilled Navy SEALs. The cream of the crop, the most highly disciplined officers and enlisted men from the Navy.

Like Tuck, the team was tired of playing pretend. They wanted to get in and do the job. But, like most missions, they didn't know when they would go, who their target would be, or where they'd have to go to take him out. Only time and their commanding officers would tell. Only when they were about two hours out would they get their final orders and all the details.

In the meantime, they'd be off duty until the following morning's PT, unless orders came in that night. It happened. But if Tuck waited around his apartment for it to come about, he'd go stir-crazy. Besides, he wanted to see O'Connell and pick up where they'd left off the night before.

Back at base, Delaney O'Connell climbed out of the pilot's seat and grabbed her flight bag. Adrenaline still thrumming through her veins, she knew going back to her apartment for the night wasn't an option.

Her co-pilot, Lt. Mark Doggett, aka K-9, fell in step beside her. "The team's headed to DD's Corral for a beer and some dancing. I know you don't usually like to hang out, but it's been a tough week. Wanna go?"

"Sure," she said, a little too quickly. Any other time, she'd have cut him off with a quick, but polite, *no*. But if she went back to her apartment alone, Tuck might show up and what good would that bring? Somehow, she'd fallen off the abstinence wagon with a vengeance and she was having a hard time getting back on.

"Great." K-9 cleared his throat. "Do you

need a ride?"

"No, thank you. I prefer to drive myself."

"Probably a good idea. These Navy guys work hard and play harder."

As well she knew. Tuck had played her in bed like a musician played an electric guitar, hitting every one of her chords like a master.

Her body quivered with remembered excitement, her core heating to combustible levels. Maybe going to the club was a bad idea. If Tuck was there…

She squared her shoulders. They didn't call her Razor for nothing. She would cut him off like she'd done so many others who'd tried getting too close. And soon. Walking away from a physical relationship was a hell of a lot easier than walking away from an emotionally involved one. Delaney refused to invest her emotions in another man with an addiction to adrenaline rushes. She'd been there once and would not go there again.

Before Tuck, she'd gone two years without a man in her life. Two years since Mad Max, Captain Chase Madden, bought it on a leadership interdiction mission in Pakistan. When a Special Forces soldier had been left behind, he'd gone back into hostile territory against his commanding officer's order. His helicopter had been shot down. Max had been injured, but was still alive until the Taliban found him and dragged him through the streets tied to the back of a truck. By the time they untied him, he'd bled out.

Delaney had been devastated. No one knew

she and Mad Max had gotten engaged two weeks prior to his deployment. And no one would, if she could help it. Being a part of the 160th Special Operations Aviation Regiment was an honor she took very seriously.

She understood her position was precarious. On more than one occasion, her CO had told her she was on probation as the only female ever entrusted with the honor of flight leader in an all-male corp. The powers that be were watching her every move. One misstep and she would be out, and she'd worked too damned hard to get here. Three years of training, and working her way up the food chain, and a rock-hard body, at least where it counted, had gotten her noticed.

Fooling around with Tuck, one of the Navy SEALs assigned to this training mission, wouldn't go over well with her commander. But the strain of anticipation and the long bout of celibacy had taken their toll on Delaney. She'd needed a release. When Tuck and Reaper offered to help her change her flat tire, she never dreamed she'd end up in bed with one of them. But those damned SEALs with their massive biceps and quads...

Holy shit. What a mistake. And Tuck would probably think their liaison meant something.

Which it didn't.

She didn't need a man in her life. Not when her missions were as dangerous as they were. And a relationship with a SEAL was as dumb as it got. Her in the Army, him in the Navy. Both deployable at a moment's notice and most likely to opposite ends of the earth. Only Kismet was what brought them together at Little Creek, Virginia, to train for a possible mission. If they deployed together, their sleeping together would only complicate matters. And she needed a clear head to complete the missions she would be responsible for flying.

Tonight, she'd tell Tuck not to expect anything. She wasn't into commitment or the long-term relationships.

Other Titles
by Elle James

Brotherhood Protector Series
Montana SEAL (#1)
Bride Protector SEAL (#2)
Montana D-Force (#3)
Cowboy D-Force (#4)
Montana Ranger (#5)
Montana Dog Soldier (#6)
Montana SEAL Daddy (#7)

Take No Prisoners Series
SEAL's Honor (#1)
SEAL's Ultimate Challenge (#1.5)
SEAL's Desire (#2)
SEAL's Embrace (#3)
SEAL's Obsession (#4)
SEAL's Proposal (#5)
SEAL's Seduction (#6)
SEAL's Defiance (#7)
SEAL's Deception (#8)
SEAL's Deliverance (#9)

Ballistic Cowboys Series
Hot Combat (#1)
Hot Target (#2)
Hot Zone (#3)
Hot Velocity (#4)

SEAL of my Own Series
Navy SEAL Survival (#1)
Navy SEAL Captive (#2)
Navy SEAL To Die For (#3)
Navy SEAL Six Pack (#4)

Thunder Horse Series
Hostage to Thunder Horse (#1)
Thunder Horse Heritage (#2)
Thunder Horse Redemption (#3)
Christmas at Thunder Horse Ranch (#4)

Covert Cowboys Inc Series
Triggered (#1)
Taking Aim (#2)
Bodyguard Under Fire (#3)
Cowboy Resurrected (#4)
Navy SEAL Justice (#5)
Navy SEAL Newlywed (#6)
High Country Hideout (#7)
Clandestine Christmas (#8)

Devil's Shroud or Deadly Series
Deadly Reckoning (#1)
Deadly Engagement (#2)
Deadly Liaisons (#3)
Deadly Allure (#4)
Deadly Obsession (#5)
Deadly Fall (#6)

Billionaire Online Dating Series
The Billionaire Husband Test (#1)
The Billionaire Cinderella Test (#2)

Hellfire Series
Hellfire, Texas (#1)
Justice Burning (#2)
Smoldering (#3)
Up in Flames (#4)

Lords of the Underworld
Witch's Initiation (#1)
Witch's Seduction (#2)
The Witch's Desire (#3)
Possessing the Witch (#4)

Demon Series
Hot Demon Nights (#1)
Demon's Embrace (#2)
Tempting the Demon (#3)

Protecting the Colton Bride
Heir to Murder
Secret Service Rescue
Tarzan & Janine
Haunted
Engaged with the Boss
Cowboy Brigade
Time Raiders: The Whisper
Bundle of Trouble
Killer Body

Operation XOXO
An Unexpected Clue
Baby Bling
Nick of Time
Under Suspicion, With Child
Texas-Sized Secrets
Alaskan Fantasy
Blown Away
Cowboy Sanctuary
Lakota Baby
Dakota Meltdown
Beneath the Texas Moon